WHEN THE FLOWERS ARE GONE

Memoir

NORMAN BEAUPRÉ

Other works by the author:

1. *L'Enclume et le couteau—the Life and Work of Adelard Coté, Folk Artist*. NMDC, Manchester, N.H., 1982. Reprint by Llumina Press, Coral Springs, FL, 2007.
2. *Le Petit Mangeur de Fleurs*, Éd. JCL, Chicoutimi, Québec, 1999.
3. *Lumineau*, Éd. JCL, Chicoutimi, Québec, 2002.
4. *Marginal Enemies*, Llumina Press, Coral Springs, FL 2004.
5. *Deux Femmes, Deux Rêves*, Llumina Press, Coral Springs, FL. 2005.
6. *La Souillonne, Monologue sur scène*, Llumina Press, Coral Springs, FL. 2006.
7. *Before All Dignity Is Lost*, Llumina Press, Coral Springs, FL. 2006.
8. *Trails Within: Meditation on the walking trails at the Ghost Ranch in Abiquiu, New Mexico*, Llumina Press, Coral Springs, FL. 2007.
9. *La Souillonne deusse*, Llumina Press, Coral Springs, FL.2008.
10. *The Boy With the Blue Cap---Van Gogh in Arles*,Llumina Press, Coral Springs, FL. 2008.
11. *Voix Francophones de chez nous---contes et histoires par Normand Beaupré et autres*, Llumina Press, Coral Springs, FL.2009.
12. *La Souillonne, Dramatic Monologue*, translated from the French by the author, Llumina Press, Coral Springs, FL2009.
13. *The Man With the Easel of Horn, the Life and Works of ÉMILE FRIANT, Llumina Press, Coral Springs, FL. 2010*
14. *The Little Eater of Bleeding Hearts*, trans. From the French by the author, Llumina Press, Coral Springs, FL. 2010.
15. *Simplicity in the Life of the Gospels---Spiritual Reflections*, Llumina Press, Coral Springs, FL. 2011.
16. *Madame Athanase T. Brindamour, raconteuse, histoires et folleries*,Llumina Press, Coral Springs, FL.2012.
17. *Cajetan, the Stargazer*, Llumina Press, Coral Springs, FL.2012.

18. *L'Étranger Extraterrestre,*Llumina Press, Plantation, FL.2013.

19. *Marie Quat'e-Poches et Sarah Foshay,* Llumina Press, Plantation, FL. 2013.

20. *The Fallen Divina, Maria Callas,* Llumina Press, Plantation, FL. 2015.

21. *Souvenances d'une Enfance Francophone Rêveuse,* Llumina Press, Plantation, FL. 2016.

22. *The Day the Horses Went to the Fair, Animal Lover and Painter, Rosa Bonheur,* LitFire Publishing, Atlanta, GA. 2017.

23. *Lucienne, la Simple d'Esprit,* LitFire Publishing, Atlanta, GA. 2017.

24. *Of Boa Constrictors, Elephants, and Imaginary Whales--- Cautionary Tales,* Stonewall Press, Bethesda, MD, 2018.

25. *[en cours/*in process] *La Souillonne et son cat'chisse en images.*

Dedication: For Paul Brown, my soft-spoken publicist, my friend and the engine that keeps me going

A SIMPLE INTRODUCTION

A few words as an introduction: When I published my Memoir or as my French publisher said *mon roman-vérité* entitled *"Le Petit Mangeur de Fleurs"*, *"The* Little Eater of Bleeding Hearts," in translation, I had several readers who kept asking me if there was going to be a follow-up to this work. They had so appreciated this memoir that they wanted more about my life and my activities. I had ended the work with a scene at Fortunes Rocks in Biddeford Pool by the seashore musing on my future and possible travels since I did not want to remain frozen in time and location, growing up with no bright future in store. I wanted to travel and write as well as explore the many opportunities that were waiting for me. I was seventeen and I planned to stop "eating little bleeding hearts", if you have read "The Little Eater", and move on to the next episodes in my life. I ended this particular work, being hungry, literally hungry as well as hungry for new adventures especially in writing.

I sought success in whatever way or venue I would be able to find since I had no heroes or human examples of men that had attained success except for a very few individuals of my ethnic group. My ethnic background was French-Québécois being of the third generation of immigrants from the Quebec province. My maternal language was French. My cultural heritage was couched in what was called Franco-American. As I have said before, I wanted to fly over the nets of cultural restraints as James Joyce said. I did not want to be identified with what was called *canuck* or one of the poor mill workers whose lot was cast in stone it seemed. How would I attain my goal as an avid wanderer in the land of the creative imagination and story-telling. As

I have said before, the human being is basically a story-teller and I wanted to adhere basically to this definition and calling. And so here is the continuation of my story as a young man growing up to full maturity.

CHAPTER ONE

Recalling the past

Recalling the past is not always easy. It can be a difficult task if one is looking for details and chronological facts and happenings. It's as if one has to look closely into one's mental files where everything is stored. Some memories are vivid while others are elusive. While my memory is good at retrieving things, it is not always faithful in retrieving details, events, and happenings. It's very good at retrieving people and their impact on me while not very helpful when it comes to remembering dates and particular moments in my life that happened years ago. There are things that cannot be erased from my mind for they cling to me like barnacles on a ship, and will not let go. I even remember the colors and design of a certain tie that I wore at my undergraduate commencement at St. Francis College, Biddeford, Maine in May 1967. I had chosen it myself. It had a swirling pattern of a deep yellow and bright red colors, and I thought it represented the school colors very well, red and gold. Although some people thought that it was a silly-looking tie, I was proud to wear it. St. Francis College, a Franciscan private institution, is a bright star in my firmament of memories. But, before I get to here, I want to go back to the ending of my book, "The Little Eater of Bleeding Hearts" where I am sitting on the seashore at Fortunes Rocks in Biddeford Pool.

As I did in "The Little Eater", I will not so much rely on chronology but on certain ideas or themes as well as events that highlighted my life at a certain time period. In that particular book I relied on relationships and certain happenings captured in the domains of women, men and words in particular. Although the design of this book will include relationships and people who touched my life, I will enlarge the scope of this memoir and include much more information about my emotional, intellectual and spiritual development. I will try to keep things in an orderly perspective as far as dates and happenings occurred in order to give the reader a sense of unstated chronology. Enough of this babbling.

The year 1964 was a watershed event for me. That's the year I was admitted as an undergraduate student at St. Francis College in Maine. Thanks to the advice of the Dean, a Franciscan called Fr. Benedict, I was able to get a student loan and planned to follow a three-year condensed baccalaureate program due to the opening of summer classes that year. I was working in the Cost Accounting Department at a local mill then. I had been married for six years and had a daughter who was five years old. The agreement with the college and my family was that I was to continue working part-time as a cost accountant and travel daily to my classes. I would save time and money by doing it in three years. Of course, it meant a lot of work and deep concentration on my studies what with the necessary readings, the term papers and the assigned research on certain subject matters. I had decided to major in English since I wanted to teach at the high school level once I graduated. However, since my French was excellent in both speaking and writing, two French professors invited me, no, convinced me to get a double major, English and French. I followed their advice thinking two majors were better than one. Since I had dreamed of getting a college education for such a long time and thought I could not afford it, I put all my energy into the pursuit of a baccalaureate. I was the first one in my family, really in the entire generation of Beauprés to go to college. My father had a six-grade education while my mother had some basic learning for a couple of years at a country school in Augusta, Maine where my grandfather Hubert had purchased a small farm after he moved from Newmarket, N.H. where he worked in a local mill after having emigrated from a small village in Quebec. He had been a farmer all of his working life before his departure from Canada and so he returned to what he loved best. My mother's family had thirteen children with one or two deaths. My mother was the thirteenth child who contracted infantile paralysis when she was but two years old. She remained a cripple all of her life with one leg shorter than the other and a deformed foot. She later got an operation on the foot that somehow reduced her infirmity allowing her to walk better rather than on the tip of her maligned foot. We her three children never thought that she was a cripple. We always knew her that way, limping along and doing her chores with a daring efficiency. None of my aunts, uncles, cousins and other relatives that I knew had a college education. I was indeed the very first one and was proud of it. Of course, I was not going to waste my time and effort in studying for a degree that I so admired and sought after. Education with its ramifications and promises meant more to me than all other pursuits. I was determined to work hard at it and not miss my chances of success since success to me did not mean money but self-improvement and self-reliance. I was determined that I would reach for the stars and not the worldly things in life. Of course, such things did matter, but were not of great importance to me. The key was opening doors and windows to the expansion of my mind and that meant getting an education. But how if one is poor and has very few resources. I wasn't really poor but my financial status was extremely low. My poor salary as a mill worker was far below average. It was as low as one gets when opportunities for advancement are dim and barely obtainable. No one wants to offer qualified opportunities to someone who has few qualifications and meager experiences in leading a productive life. I knew I had the intellectual qualifications and capacities for success in life, but I needed a chance to prove myself. Who was going to give it to me? I realized that I had to get it myself and no one was going to offer it to me on a silver platter. I had to create opportunities myself by scratching the surfaces of possibilities and hunting down all possibilities and that took an educated mind. That's the road I was determined to take. The pittances and strife of mill labor and shoe shop work were not going to suffice. I knew that. I had watched both my father and my mother as well as many of my relatives struggle in those confines only to get very little in life. Bare survival even to the point of losing their jobs during the Great Depression with the result, for my parents, of losing their newly purchased property, our home on Cleaves Street. That would be the greatest disappointment in my mother's life. My mother and father managed, but they would struggle all of their lives trying to rise above all missed opportunities coupled with reversals that came their way. My father was by no means an example of success for me. He was the poor lamb that is shorn by bosses and factory owners who are out to get the profits they sought over the tired and depleted strength of the common laborer. I must admit that I admired, at least, the courage and the submission to everyday struggles of my father. He never got depressed and never felt cheated out of possible success. He was like Job who was patient and persistent in his adherence to an Old Testament demanding God. My father was a religious man. That is why he survived the reversals that life offered him. I truly believe that. Of course, growing up, I did not realize the struggles and difficulties my parents had to go through. The family was the glue that held the five of us together in a secure and loving way. My two sisters were very close to me. They called me Nomun as many of my relatives did. That was their way of being intimate and caring.

I need to backtrack at this juncture of my story since I have left the reader between the ending of the first installment, so-to-speak, of my memoir, "The Little Eater", and the continuation of my story before I went to college. Otherwise, there would be a large enough gap in telling my entire story.

I left the reader at the seashore at Fortunes Rocks meandering in my thoughts and not being too sure about my success in life. Would I be a writer, would I achieve success in life, whatever success is. I certainly did not want to spend the rest of my life struggling with the vagaries of the uneducated attempts of a mill worker whose fate is couched in a predetermined heritage of the offspring of Québécois immigrants with little promise of a bright future. But, what awaited me? Would I fall in the worn out shoes of the downtrodden mill worker? Would I be ever blessed with rare opportunities of making my own blissful way in life or would I be condemned like Sisyphus to an eternal downhill fate accepting defeat and loss of opportunities. Would I like Camus's Greek mythical hero keep climbing the slope only to fall back down constantly. Camus's assessment that Sisyphus remains happy was not my way of seeing things. If I happen to climb the slope of success, I would remain there by vanquishing the struggles of the poor sacrificial lamb, *le mouton*, as the ancestors used to call the common laborer who has no goals in life but to work on a farm and eke out an existence. There is an expression in French that goes like this, *se faire manger la laine sur le dos* (to let the wool be eaten off one's back) which means to let oneself be abused. I certainly did not want that. I was determined not to fail and reach my goal of a successful individual who attains something worthwhile in his lifetime. What would that be, I asked myself sitting there on a large rock overlooking the ocean at Fortunes Rocks. As I said at the end of the memoir, I was hungry, hungry for food and hungry for intellectual pursuits.

CHAPTER TWO

My vocation

At the age of twelve and a half, I followed the repeated advice of my seventh grade teacher, a Brother of the Sacred-Heart, and joined that community of religious teachers in Winthrop, Maine, My grandmother Beaupré thought I was much too young to leave home. However, I decided to leave Biddeford and my family to pursue my vocation. That's how it was known then. That was January 11, 1948. After three years of training and education, I was named postulant and six months later I was sent to the novitiate in Ancienne-Lorette, Quebec. I only stayed there two months due to a deep sense of loneliness and longing to go home.

After I left the novitiate in the fall of 1951, my first job was in a shoe shop, the Kesslen, in Kennebunk. I was given the learner's task of pulling tacks from a wooden last in order to remove the finished shoe and depositing it on the wooden rack. It was a monotonous and simplistic task that bored me to death. It paid the minimum wage of 55 cents an hour. I got a weekly salary of $21.45 after deductions. I gave my salary to my mother. She allowed me $2.00 for my own expenses. I did not have a car. It did not matter since I did not know how to drive. I walked a lot. Since Kennebunk was some eight miles away, I paid $2.00 a week for a ride to work. I felt that I was not earning much with little money in my pocket at the end of the week. That was the case of many young men like me who had to suffer the consequence of being poor and formally uneducated beyond high school. I did not have any friends since I had not attended high school in my community. I felt isolated and alone. Besides, I was shy and not ready to accept a world that was new to me since I had been away four years living the community life where everything was planned and orchestrated for you. I did not have to worry nor plan for anything except to march to the daily orders of the day. It was a life committed to prayer, daily exercise, school work, and three meals a day with a collation at four o'clock in the afternoon. I adapted very well to community life. I was hardly thirteen years old when I entered the Juniorate of the Brothers of the Sacred-Heart in Winthrop, Maine. I had many fellow teenagers who became my brothers and filled the gap of not having a single brother back home. I enjoyed their company and thrived in it. I learned to play sports such as volley ball, tennis, touch football, hand ball and spiral ball. The one sport I did not like was baseball since I had never learned to throw the ball like a boy and had no agility to go at bat and hit the dreadful ever fast ball coming at me that I feared most of the time. I remember one time standing in left field with a glove in my hand. A hit came in my direction and someone hollered, "It's your ball." I tried catching it but the ball struck me in the left eye. I was left in pain for an entire week. No wonder, I told myself, that I was chosen last as the teams were assembled. I just wished that I could be exempted from playing baseball, but everyone had to participate in the sport want to or not. The Director ordered it that way and he was a true disciplinarian. He was a kind man, a hard-working man and an individual who played the organ as well as the piano but could not carry a tune. He had a big job on his hands molding and shaping spiritually, intellectually and I might say, emotionally and psychologically, a group of some twenty boys as well as a small congregate of scholastics, young brothers who had just come back from the novitiate to study for their normal school diplomas. I must admit that the years spent in Winthrop were some of the most cherished years of my life. They were years of self-discipline by following the rule of a community of religious individuals, years of making friends and a time for growing up with intellectual opportunities. I worked hard, prayed hard and learned hard.

Since the Juniorate was an old farm that was being re-utilized as a training school and farm with some animals and a huge garden as well as a canning house, we all participated in the tasks of maintaining the farm with the experienced help of an old brother called Brother Oscar who was a French Canadian. He was a short man and quite pudgy. He was quite the character and he made us laugh every time we worked with him in the garden. He was a jovial and even-tempered sort. We even helped in the haying season. What I especially liked in the early fall was apple picking. There was a large orchard of Macintosh apples. I just loved sinking my teeth into one of them when we were given a break. They were fresh, crunchy and sublimely delicious. I learned to swim in the Maranacook Lake where we had a path dug and groomed by predecessors. In the summertime, we often went there for swimming and picnicking. It was indeed a time of relaxation and joy. Yes, the years spent at Winthrop were indeed memorable ones. I still remember that time vividly.

After the Juniorate there was the short-lived time at the Novitiate in Canada. I left the Novitiate because I felt alone and somewhat depressed by the fact that very few novices spoke to me and no one bothered with me except the master of novices, Brother Sylvio. But he was a very busy man. I understood that most of them were Québécois who considered me a foreigner. I truly missed my colleagues in Winthrop. We were like a family. That's how I considered the matter. What I truly missed was Winthrop and not really my own family in Biddeford.

Well, returning to Biddeford, my home town, I felt somewhat out of place since I had no friends and no plans for a future that was yet to be determined. Fortunately, I had my immediate family and some relatives that received me with open arms. However, I felt alone and without any sense of direction in my young life. I was sixteen years old and knew nothing about making friends, girls, sex, and other things that young men know. I had been sheltered and kept apart from the world, the term often used by religious men and women to designate the world of dangerous temptations and material dreams. I had been trained to become a religious brother in a particular community given to religious vocation, a calling that required religious convictions and a sense of dedication to the community rule. The formation of a religious meant years of education, retreats, daily prayers with daily mass, as well as following examples of charitable works and the living of one's faith. It wasn't hard for me since I was open to such activities. I was altogether pliable, malleable, and obedient and open to any rule that was established by the community. I was a true candidate for religious life. Spirituality for me was a state of soul and a goal that blended well with my penchants and my disposition for the monastic life. I have to give credit to all the religious brothers who helped in my formation at Winthrop since I became sensitive to and appreciative of my growing up in a family of men that somehow replaced my own family back home. I had to learn to become adaptable to a life of total personal freedom except that freedom is not always completely free. Freedom is ever linked to prescriptions of home and the community one lives in. There are laws and rules everywhere and in all things. My spiritual self did not change. I carried with me the mark of the convinced Christian as well as the vestiges of self-discipline that never faded and never disappeared from my character and my sensitive if not delicate personality. Yes, I had somewhat of a delicate personality. People said that I mirrored the personality of a young lady. I had the female tendencies of delicate behavior and shy resonance. Some even said that I did not show manly characteristics like throwing a ball the way a male does, walking forcefully like a John Wayne, or swearing like a man and even drinking and partying like many men do. Yes, I was careful to respect comeliness and appearances. I stayed away from gruffness and manly boldness. I was afraid of being a sissy when people saw the way I behaved although I was not a sissy. I did not want to be one. I merely wanted to be myself.

Since I already had my high school diploma, I did not have to attend high school once I was back home. So, I did not have to go to school dances, play sports and fraternize with other young men. I was on my own and lived in a kind of cocoon that protected me from outward manly behavior and bold activities. I was old enough to reject conformity and adhere to my own set of rules. However, I did feel somewhat strange in a milieu that did not invite behavioral differences. I didn't care. I was going to live my own life although at times I did feel somewhat lonely and craving for companionship. My sisters had their own lives, their own friends, and their own desires. I did not associate too much with them except that I looked to them to show me the way to uncover the deep reliance on one's self and the inner struggles that come with being and feeling alone. My parents did not interfere in my life nor did they show any understanding of my circumstances and my predicament. I realized that I had a strong will and acted the way I wanted and made decisions in whatever way I could. One thing for sure, I dreaded humiliation and inner pain. I did not want to suffer the loss of self-reliance and self-pride. No one was going to laugh at me. I wasn't going to let anyone call me queer, whatever that term meant. No one.

Certain things are private and cannot be revealed. That is why in protecting the deepest layer of my sense of privacy. I will not get into the sexual dimensions of my life.

I must say that I had certain desires or affinities for the male gender. I remember when I was in Winthrop, we went swimming at the lake and afterwards, we changed into our dry clothes in the makeshift compartments that had fiberboard walls with small holes in them probably made with nails extracted when being taken from their location. It happened that I became a peeping-tom and one day and watched an older juvenist taking off his swimsuit, drying himself and then touching his penis so that it became what I then called inflated, bigger and bigger. I was startled to see that some white oozy stuff came out and fell on the ground. He then hurried to finish dressing and I did the same thing getting out somewhat puzzled by what I had seen. Somewhat later after our meal together while no one was watching, I slipped into the compartment where the white stuff lay on the dirt floor. I bent down and touched it with my finger trying to make out what that was. It was gooey and I did not want it glued to my finger. I wiped the finger on my pants and rushed out of there. It was much later that I got to know that it was called sperm and by the process of masturbation, such a fluid came out whenever the organ known as the penis was stimulated. I took a liking to that young man and had wet dreams just thinking about him in my dreams. That was part of growing up I was told by Father Confessor. I imagined that I had to confess this happening since I considered it a sin. The Calvinistic or rather the Jansenistic conservative streak never left my conscience and pervaded my thoughts in the process of self-examination whenever we were asked to do so. This was part of my traditional values. I still have the vestiges of that. It will never go away, I don't think. It's part of my inclination to remain the spiritually-bound self that I am. I can't help it. It's an integral part of me that refuses to die or fade away. You see, certain things are that way. They cling to the inner self and simply hang on to a sense of intimate privacy that one has sheltered all along. I truly believe that this has been part and parcel of our French heritage, being disciplined by rules and regulations be they civil, church related, or otherwise. Religion was a strong factor in my life and it still is. I recognize that it's due not only to my personal beliefs and convictions but to my entire way of seeing and doing things based irrevocably on my heritage. I know that I could get away from all of this and even deny it but that would mar if not dissipate my identity as a Franco-American. All in all, I could very well deny and discard my maternal language, my ethnic values, and live a life devoid of differences but that would not be me since I cannot do that. I thought of it at one time growing up, but then I told myself I could not erase my birth, my race, my gender and my deep-embedded values, including my heritage, with which I was born. My identity is really all that I have that is important and real. I don't want to mess with my identity and try to become someone else in the process. I do not want to fly over my ethnic nets[James Joyce], but rather I want to enhance my ethnic values by living them faithfully. That's what I have learned over the course of my growing up over many years. I suppose that is what maturity does for you.

CHAPTER THREE

My studies

I am now at the junction of growing up as a child then a teenager and then reaching gradually maturity. It wasn't always an easy passage. I had many a hurdle to encounter and jump over. First there was the challenge of finding my niche in life. Was I going after a career, or simply a job that would put money in my pocket and allow me to simply enjoy life as it unfolded. I told myself that I wasn't going to be a passive bystander in life. I was going to aim at becoming better educated and seek some kind of a career be it in business or in teaching. Teaching appealed to me ever since I had joined the community of the Brothers of the Sacred-Heart. That was their vocation and it was mine also. It was a genuine calling that reverberated in my thoughts and in my heart. I knew that I had the capabilities and the will to succeed in such a calling. Besides, I told myself that I had the intellectual abilities to deal with the challenges of learning and teaching, I was convinced of that. And so, I embarked on my journey of finding the right road that would open up for me both success and fulfillment. But, how do I start, I asked myself. It's not an easy question when you have no direct lead and no one to guide you. My father couldn't nor could or would any relative since they did not have the skills nor the experience. I knew that I would have to explore alone and learn to follow both my instincts and my adventurous energies. At time, I was a bit afraid of wandering through difficult paths like introducing myself to a businessman, a community leader or a manager of some firm. I knew that I had to meet the challenge of self-introduction if I wanted to succeed if I wanted to go where I the opportunities lay.

My first venture was with the local manager of the Metropolitan Life Insurance. I had read in the local newspaper that the firm was looking for young men who were willing to learn the trade and even travel to New York to attend some workshops in order to be trained as the firm so forcefully wanted. After some words of introduction, the local manager asked me if I had any experience in selling. I told him that I had none. He then replied that I needed that in order to qualify for the trainee opening. "But, how am I going to get it if people like you do not offer it to me. I have to start somewhere," I told him. "Well," he replied, "go and start by getting a selling job in a store or any other place somewhere." I was stunned by his reply. How would I learn if no one gave me the opportunity to learn and be trained in a given position? Besides, I did not want a job as a clerk in a store selling stuff. I felt deceived and misled by the Metropolitan manager and his company. What did he expect of me? Why did he advertise in the local paper that they wanted young men to be trained as insurance representatives? What did it take to get the offer? I felt that the manager did not believe in my capabilities and that my ethnic background hindered me in that he probably thought that I was one of those canucks, neither intellectually gifted nor socially connected to the proper sources in the community. I left the office totally disenchanted with business ventures. Why did they advertise if they did not want young men like me? I kept telling myself that businessmen like the Metropolitan manager were discriminative and blind to potential qualities in an individual. That was one hurdle that I knew I had to overcome in the future. I knew then that I had to learn through experience and not necessarily through books. Book learning is fine but it must be coupled with practical experience otherwise you are bound to be deceived.

Mill work is not easy. I mean working in the mills such as Bates and Pepperell in Biddeford. They were the staple employers in our mill towns. Many immigrants from Canada had no other options for work with a salary. Most of them left the farm struggling with depleted crops, a lack of knowledge of crop rotation and much-needed fertilizers. Besides, most families were large families sometimes numbering eighteen to twenty-two children. When you realize you cannot survive under taxing conditions, you get the hell out of there. The answer at that time was emigrate where there are job opportunities for both men and women including children. New England received thousands of immigrants in the early 20th Century. They came in droves and established themselves with their families in ethnic neighborhoods that became little Canadas. It was hard work but these people learned fast, job requirements as well as language. They put in long hours and deprived themselves of luxuries and travel except to return to their native villages once a year much like a pilgrimage. Tradition, heritage and ethnic values were considered viable venues in life. Everyone shared and everyone adhered to their Catholic faith with conviction and ardor. Very few considered living outside of these ramparts of beliefs and convictions. They believed in educating their children given the time and the opportunity when their salaries at the mill were not direly needed. They had pulled themselves up by their boot straps into a less demanding life of hard work and scrimping. Many of them dreamed of a better life of some comfort and ease. I was of the third generation of Canadian immigrants to the States. Both my father and mother were born in the United States. My maternal grandparents as well as my paternal grandfather came from the Quebec province. My paternal grandmother was born in Maine of parents of Québécois roots. I shared their heritage, their language and their faith. I was not a rebellious child nor was ever I difficult youngster. I minded my elders and obeyed my teachers. I followed the path already established by my predecessors and looked forward to leading a harmonious and well-ordered life since it was expected of me. I went to a parochial Catholic school named St André's and joined many in large classes that were taught by the Presentation of Mary nuns except for the boys who once having arrived in the fifth grade, were taught by the Brothers of the Sacred-Heart. That's where I found my invitation to join their community in Winthrop, Maine.

To continue my story after I had worked in the shoe shops and the Pepperell mills soon to be followed by the Saco-Lowell Shops, makers of textile machinery, I continued to explore my options in the search of a job that would satisfy my quest for success in life. Once I had left the difficult laborious charge of the carding department where I had lost fourteen pounds lifting and changing the huge cotton rolls on the assigned cards, thirteen of them, I looked to other opportunities in my job search. I told myself that I wasn't going to spend the rest of my existence working in the mill like so many of my relatives and friends had done for thirty, forty and even fifty years. All they received at retirement was a gold watch and sometimes the pittance of a bonus with a pitiful and ironic, thank you. Success for me was much more than that. Success was something earned by strong-willed determination, an energetic wish to make things work for me and above all a desire to overcome whatever hindrances on my path in life. A tall order but I maintained my goal in a forceful and determine way. I did not know what that would entail but I was willing and determined to reach that goal whatever it was, education and opportunities given to me whatever they would be. I was not satisfied with mediocre opportunities. I wanted more than that. I wanted opportunities that would open doors and windows to a greater expansion in my life. I was willing to take chances. Sometimes I wonder how I managed to throw myself into situations that I had to face in order to grow into the mature stage of my life. Determination is a prime factor in the pursuit of plans and executions. No matter what, I was determined to succeed and go on to higher levels of success whatever that was. My determination led me to not only fly over my ethnic net but to soar high and wide. I would take every opportunity presented to me no matter if it meant a daring look into what could possibly happen as long as I played it safe. I was daring in my thoughts and in my actions but remained timid in my approach to things. I had to get over that, I told myself.

After I left my job at the mill, I just told my boss, "I quit." My mother did not speak to me for days because I did not have another job in view and she dreaded the loss of a salary. My next job venture was at the Saco-Lowell plant in the industrial arts and design department under the supervision of Dave Walley, a jovial man who delegated rather than order people around. My immediate boss was Fern Loranger, a kind and knowledgeable man who taught me several skills such as collating forms, paper-cutting machine skills, and hand-operated printing. I enjoyed that job since it had a variance of assignments. The several employees there became my friends. After a year and a half, I left

Saco-Lowell and returned to the Pepperell mill but not as a mill worker but an office worker in the blanket finishing department. I was in charge of ordering supplies and maintaining inventories. I worked under the supervision of Ernest Martel, a dedicated and understanding man who seemed always in a hurry. Sitting at her desk facing mine was Lucinda Lord, a refined, pleasant and mild-mannered lady in her mid-fifties. We had short but pleasant conversations together. She was unmarried and living with her brother in Kennebunk. I admired her refined and educated ways of speaking and doing things. She would have made an excellent ambassador, I thought. She had that disposition and human skills. I truly enjoyed this job since I felt comfortable as an office worker. I might have been considered somewhat of a snob but that was not my intent nor my disposition. I simply wanted to climb the ladder of success in a society that called for refinement and educated skills. After all, I was definitely not *un canuck manqué*, a failed Frenchman. I wanted to be somebody and not a creature of low expectations and shabby dreams. I must admit that I was a person of a creative imagination and lofty dreams. I told myself that a person without dreams and high expectations was not going to succeed well in the world, certainly not in a society that respected these qualities. Was my nose up in the air? I don't think so. *Fierté* is the word I would use which means pride but a cultural pride. That's the way I would translate it.

After my three years in the blanket finishing department, I found myself in the cost accounting department. I never liked math and accounting, but here was an opportunity that offered me the chance of advancement. I could learn the exigencies of the job and in a short time, I did under the kind and masterful direction of my boss, Lennie Burke. He taught me how to set a large sheet of a particular cost accounting product with overhead costs, such as a specific blanket with its packaging and any other detailed demands by the purchaser. I learned the various implications of doing cost accounting even though I had very little background and experience in accounting. What I truly liked about the job was my checking with the blanket finishing department employees about various products associated with a given blanket such as binding, ticketing, special packaging and other required items for a particular company. That's what I conveyed to my boss as he was seeking specific information for a particular company that was ordering large amounts of blankets for its stores. I was also given the task of calling the New York sales office to determine the exact specifications for the packaging of a particular blanket such as a receiving blanket or a lovely baby blanket with all the trimmings. I truly enjoyed these calls since I began to think that I was connecting with high business and people who dealt with corporate America. I was learning something that was above and beyond my circle of restrictive possibilities. I was flying above the nets.

My salary was very low but I managed to eke out a living with my small family. However, I still dreamed of getting a college degree. That came with my decision to attend St. Francis College in 1964. I had asked for a decent raise and all the company offered me was five dollars. I was making fifty dollars a week then. Then came my decision to leave the job and go to college. Well, when my supervisor told the company Vice-President in charge of accounting about my leaving, I was then offered a forty-five dollar raise. I refused telling them that I was going to study for my bachelor's degree. They were amazed at my refusal, but I was determined to get an education no matter what. I suppose that they thought they were losing a good asset to their cost accounting department so they offered me the opportunity to work part-time at my present job. That was fine with me since that added money to my budget. So I went to classes every day and put in twenty hours per week at my job as cost accountant. I did that for two years until I accepted the offer of working in the language lab aiding the language and audio/visual Director with students who were learning a foreign language. Most of them were studying French. That was up my alley as they say.

I was really in my glory realizing my dream of a college education. I took six courses, eighteen credit hours per semester. That was the maximum allowed. I followed the humanities curriculum which comprised of history, algebra and trigonometry, English, economics, theology, philosophy and, of course a foreign language. Of course, French was definitely not a foreign language for me. I had very good teachers. There was one, a Franciscan, Fr. Raymond Lagacé, who became my favorite professor of French civilization, culture and history. He had just returned from Paris where he attended the Sorbonne and had delivered an oral thesis on Albert Camus for a final exam. He was truly in his element when it came to French. Many students in his classes were Franco-Americans like me. Our maternal language was French. I learned very fast and with an intellectual ardor that was reflected in my grades. I simply loved French and it's cultural, historical and linguistic values. I realized that what I was undertaking was my dream come true, an education that would enrich my life and at the same time open doors in the market of jobs for the future. I was often placed on the Dean's list every semester since my grade average was always way above 3.0. The only "C" I ever had was in my algebra and trigonometry class. I had expected that because math had never been my forté. And, to think that I had succeeded so well in my cost accounting job. That was because it was an applied math experience. The thought of a x b + c2= whatever was Greek to me. Algebra was too abstract a concept for me. I could deal with philosophy, economics theories, historical data and abstract concepts in theology, but algebra and I were not in the best of terms, one could say.

I also enjoyed my English classes which would become my second major. I took a poetry class from a young professor name Al Poulin, a very bright and energetic person. It was the first time that I wrote poetry. One poem was "Danaus Archippus"(the Monarch Butterfly) that was included in the students' monthly magazine which gave me a sense of literary pride and accomplishment. From another professor, the dean of English teachers, Mister Hennedy, an intellectual giant in his academic element but a severe-looking man, since he always had somewhat of a frown on his face, I took several courses. I signed up for Shakespeare, Blake, Wordsworth, and world playwrights as well as Chaucer. I took two semesters of Shakespeare's plays, one semester on his tragedies and the following semester on his comedies. Each one consisted of two term papers. That was an awful lot of work considering I had three other courses to deal with as well as some twenty hours of job work. One of the humanities courses taught by four professors was called "Christian Literature." I especially enjoyed one of them, Professor Ruth Rosenau, a teacher of German, who taught us Dante's Purgatorio and Inferno. She was originally from Germany and had survived WWII. She revealed to us her adventures of danger and intrigue as she enlightened us with her stories of Nazi attempts to capture Jews like her. She had hidden herself in a closet for days. She also dealt with Stalin's attempts to enlist workers for his cause and she told us that one way of overcoming the effects of vodka was to drink olive oil before being forcibly given the liquor. They were trying to get some much desired information out of them, she said. She related her war experiences to Dante's Purgatory and Hell writings. For me, that was an enlightening part of the course. It brought back to mind my memories of WWII that I had experienced as a child growing up in Biddeford.

All of my days were full to the brim with my studies, work and other responsibilities. I was indeed challenged, but I fully enjoyed what I was doing and delighted in the thought that I was nearing my goal of a college education. Education for me meant that my mind and my heart were being filled not only with information, data and cumulative knowledge but it was offering me fulfillment as a young man and as a human being on a venture of creativity and intellectual growth. The day came when I graduated magna cum laude and grasped my diploma with open hands and delight for I had truly worked hard for it. What was I going to do now was the question that I asked myself at the beginning of my last semester. I resolved not to teach at the high school level since I told myself that I did not want to be a cop, a disciplinarian and watchdog. I considered the task of teaching teenagers as daunting and unenviable due to the fact that I was not prepared to do so. I thought of the college level as a more fruitful endeavor what with advanced education and a chance once more to study and learn. I submitted my application for graduate studies to Yale and the University of New Hampshire. I received from Yale the ubiquitous card of refusal. I was invited to an interview with a French professor at UNH. I thought that the interview went sour when he asked me about my skills in French and told me right then and there that he thought I had very little chance of succeeding in the course offering because my level of high quality in French looked poor and uninviting. I was going to ask him why but then it came to me that his judgment was based on his discriminatory assessment of my ethnic background, the canuck branding of Franco-Americans. That made me inferior to more sophisticated and polished students of French culture and language. Therefore, I was not admitted nor did I desire to be admitted to the UNH graduate program in French studies. I thought that it was strange that the interviewer had a French name and came from a New England town and was most probably a Franco-American like me. I realized that he had very little more sensitivity toward an ethnic confrère. That was one incident when I realized that discrimination by fellow Francos like Mister Interviewer could and would creep up occasionally in my life. However, one of my French professors suggested that I apply to Brown University since two alumni of St. Francis had been admitted there and were in the process of finishing their course work. They were at the threshold of their doctoral dissertation. I asked myself why not. I was truly determined to pursue graduate studies that would open doors to college teaching. Of course I did not fully realize that such a decision would require my moving away from Biddeford. I had never moved out of my hometown before except to go to Quebec. I had never really traveled much either. I had never been to Paris. That was another dream of mine.

I was admitted at Brown but I then realized that tuition was expensive, $4,000 at that time, in 1967. I was about to turn down Brown's offer when one Friday afternoon I received call from the chairman of the graduate French department, Professor Kuhn, asking me if I would consider accepting a National Defense Act Fellowship in the French graduate program. I needed to give him my answer right away. Without any hesitation I replied, "Yes." There was joy in my heart, the joy of yet another step in my success. However the joy was mitigated by some apprehension. I had to tell my wife that we would be moving to Rhode Island in late summer. She answered, "What?" I explained to her that this move would be the key to my academic success. She consented since she knew that I was on the path of my dream. She had gone back to work while I was at St. Francis since our income was low then. She went back to the mill in the blanket department folding receiving blankets for babies. Everyone loved her because she was a very good and conscientious worker. We lived a very moderate life then never spending a lot on any expense. We did not crave for material things such as a big car, expensive vacations or the best of clothes. We managed and we learned to make do with what we had. We had very little money in the bank. With the money we had we always said that we would save it for one day we would want to buy a house, our first home that we would call our own. Neither parents, mine nor hers had ever owned a home. They lived in a rent all their lives, a sign of the working class destiny.

And so, we moved to Rhode Island in August of 1967 after my first trip to Providence in order to find an available rent. After several inquiries, I found one on Rochambeau Avenue not too far from the university. It was a two-story house with two rents with the first one being vacant since the students who rented it had left and gone on some kind of research project. The lady who owned the property could only be reached by phone. I agreed to take the rent without seeing it thinking that it would serve our purpose. It looked good from the outside and peering through some windows I thought it was good enough for the three of us. Besides, I was in somewhat of a hurry since there was packing to be done and goodbyes to be made. Our friends and relatives could not exactly make out my plans to advance my education some distance away and without a job and a salary. The NDEA fellowship did come with a monthly stipend, enough to pay the rent and buy groceries. One look at the interior of the rent revealed to us that a lot of work was in store. The bathroom was filthy, the refrigerator had been painted black and the walls needed painting. We did not like the colors at all. We had the movers bring the refrigerator in the back hallway. Once in, we heaved a very long sigh. I then called the owner and asked her for paint. She sent us to a retailer who sold low-priced paint. There weren't too many colors to choose from. I then decided to use color tints for icing since we were buying water based paint. It worked.

The first thing we did was to clean the bathroom. The floor was filthy. I took a pail full of hot water and threw it on the floor and then I let it soak for a while. Then I began scrubbing and scraping until my hands turned red. My wife and I worked like dogs painting ceilings first then the four rooms. It took us an entire week but we succeeded in making the rent livable and practically spanking new. With our furniture in place and the curtains up in the windows, we told ourselves that we had done a fantastic job. When the students who had the rent before us came to collect some of their belongings, they were awed by the transformation. Sitting up in bed watching television that evening, I told my wife that we should have billed the owner for all the labor that we had put in, at least not pay the rent for one month. But, we were honest folks and I did not even mention this to the Jewish lady who owned the house. Besides, I never saw her. I mailed the rent to her address each month. We made arrangement for school for our daughter who was then eight years old. She walked to elementary school every day with her mother. Holy Family Catholic School it was called. It was there that our daughter made her first encounter with a black student. Our community back home had no blacks. She came home one day during her first week of school and told my wife that there were students in her grade that had chocolate milk skin. My wife was greatly amused at her revelation. She smiled and explained to her that they were real people like us and that she had to treat them as friends, white and black.

I had to familiarize myself with the Brown campus and learn the ins and outs of graduate school. It was quite an experience for me since I was not used to such a well-known and largely populated school. There were students from many parts of the world. Students who had attended famous schools such as Princeton, Yale, University of Pittsburg and even some international schools. I was like a country bumpkin out of his cabbage patch into a garden of exquisite sophistication. There were so many things that I had to learn in order to feel comfortable with myself and my surroundings. In French it is often called *se sentir bien dans sa peau*. I did it through sheer volition and determination.

I started feeling more comfortable when I realized that I was part of the Francophone world and speaking French was natural for *moi*. Everyone had to undergo an interview with Professor Sagan, a man originally from France, to determine if the student was proficient in French or not. I had no problem and the professor even complimented me on my ability to speak French. I told him that French was my maternal language. He did not realize that there were many Franco-Americans like me whose everyday language was French. A lot of times people equated us with canucks who were dumb and uneducated. I became somewhat the cultural ambassador for Franco-Americans on campus. I wasn't haughty about it, simply *fier*, proud that I was playing a part in educating people as I was being educated by Brown University.

Some of the graduate courses were enjoyable while there were a few that I found difficult and very challenging to my undergraduate knowledge. For example, most of the students in my group had a better facility with languages and their roots. They were also more knowledgeable about cultural history of many countries and, of course they had traveled more than I had. I realized that my education at the undergraduate level was more limited than that of better known schools like the Ivy League schools. However, I learned by sheer dint of immersing myself in books and my studies diligently. We had some visiting professors who came with outstanding credentials and academic capabilities. One came from the UK and had spent his entire graduate time learning about the epic of *La Chanson de Roland*. He taught part of the Middle Ages curriculum. I thought that this course was at times boring always on the same epic poem with amusing if not tiring details of the epic. To me it seemed that he had spent most of his education of the same topic. I suppose that is the way of British higher education. Another visiting professor was a French native who taught us 20th Century poetry. I liked his approach to poetry since he told us that he was a published poet himself. He loved Mallarmé and his symbolist poetry, and so when it came time to write my required paper for this class I selected Mallarmé and some of his poems such as *L'après-midi d'un faune*, a difficult poem to analyze and fully understand. Some students wanted the translation of Mallarmé's poems but the professor told us that it was very difficult to translate his work due to phonetic ambiguities. Having already mastered the French language, I had no great difficulties in dealing with symbolism and Mallarmé's poetic masterpiece. I got an A+ for the course. I never got an A+ before. Besides, I did not know that college professors gave out A+ grades. Of course he was a visiting professor, a poet who recognized my strengths with the French language. I felt that I had demonstrated that I wasn't canuck after all.

One course with which I had great difficulties was a course taught by a professor who belonged outside the French department. He was teaching in the department of what I would call roots of languages. He knew Latin, German and French as well as Italian and probably other languages. He was a tall, stern, haughty and demanding teacher. He tended to favor younger male students. I was an older student so I was not one who fell into his favored category. I could sense that after a few weeks in his class. He taught us the roots of the French language and required that we familiarize ourselves with Latin. All the other students were quite familiar with Latin but I wasn't. I had to buy a Latin basic language book. So, besides having to deal with my courses, I was trying to learn Latin. The professor was of little help since he never injected explanations about Latin and simply expected us to know everything there is to know about Latin. The reason he expected us to know Latin was because he gave us each a project for this class. Most students already had taken undergraduate courses on the topic of Latin as the root of French. I hadn't and I felt lost. The project was the selection of a text in Middle Ages literature written in Medieval French. We had to give the precise evolution of every word from Latin to contemporary French citing the actual text where each step of the evolution took place. It required a lot of research and several visits to the library. I forced myself to learn more and more about Latin to French. Although interesting and challenging, the project, to me, was not only demanding of my time and energy, but excruciatingly painful for my intellect and learning capabilities. I did manage to finish my project and finally submitted it to Professor S. The final exam was another hurdle for me but I did it and got a B- for the course. I was so glad to get rid of *mon épine*, this thorn that kept me awake at night.

Besides my coursework, I had to demonstrate proficiency with German and another romance language. For German I took a class in the German department which I found exasperatingly difficult but attainable for a B grade. As for the other romance language I took a workshop in Italian. I found Italian easier since it was of the same root category as French. I also had learned some Italian by listening to while enjoying Verdi's and Puccini's operas. I passed the written exam and jumped right back into my course work. By then, I had met every daunting challenge given to me at the graduate level. I was determined to succeed in my pursuit of the highest academic degree, the Ph.D. When I agreed to accept the NDEA fellowship it was for the doctoral program. I had no other choice even though I never considered this level of education before. I had to accomplish what I was destined for since I had the drive and challenge presented to me on a platter of impending success. My pride and my volition would not allow me to fail. Failure was out of the question for me as a Franco-American. I would show them all that I was certainly not a canuck after all.

Another professor that I had was Professor Beverly R., a Princeton graduate, a somewhat snobbish, somewhat pretentious man but a lover of nature especially of birds. His expertise was 17th Century literature and his doctoral dissertation was on the fabulist, LaFontaine. I don't remember his course too well except that it did not inspire me to further study classic literature. He did not leave much of an impression on me. I even said that I would never have him as a director of my dissertation. What an ironic thought. I'll get back to him later.

It was the policy of the French studies department to allow students to go right through the program without going for the master's degree stage. I opted to go for my masters and obtain my degree before advancing to the doctoral level. Having taken a course on *ennui* with the chairman of our department, Professor Kuhn, I decided to write my thesis on ennui in the 19th Century, specifically on the romantic poet Lamartine. *Ennui dans les romans de Lamartine* was the title of my master's thesis. I truly enjoyed Professor Kuhn. He later died of the Legionaire disease. Yet another professor that I got to know was a 17th Century specialist, Professor Hunter K., I took a course with him on classical theater that included the famous three, Corneille, Racine and Molière. For my term paper I selected Corneille and his tragedies although I truly liked Racine and his much beloved play *Phèdre*. His language is considered by many as sublime poetry and parts of his classical theater include such onomatopoetic lines as *Quels sont ces serpents qui sifflent sur nos têtes.* I will never forget that line. I did quite well with my paper and got an "A" for it. The Professor even wrote at the end of my paper that I should consider expanding on my paper and write my dissertation on Corneille. That was an interesting idea but I had not considered writing on 17th Century literature. I preferred the French romantic and symbolist literature as well as French contemporary poetry. I remember at one time I had so enjoyed 20th Century theatre and Henry de Montherlant's plays that I told my friend, Roger Normand, given the opportunity, I would select Montherlant's *Le Cardinal d'Espagne* as the topic of my doctoral dissertation. I truly loved the highly charged dramatic tension between Cardinal Cisneros the haughty and vain cleric and *Jeanne la Folle*, the

Queen of Castille and Aragon, called *Juana la Loca* . However, finding a particular topic for a doctoral dissertation and beginning from scratch was determinately not only challenging but time consuming. I wanted to obtain my doctorate sooner than later. I wanted to get a job teaching at a college and earn enough money to live on and eventually buy a home. I already had done research on Corneille and I figured that all I had to do was to expand on the paper I had written, This was a practical thing for me. It was the right thing and the right time to do so. When time came to propose the topic for my dissertation, I decided to concentrate of Corneille's classical tragedies. My topic became, *La Notion de bassesse dans le théâtre de Pierre Corneille (1633-1651)*.

I finished my course work, moved out of our rent and said goodbye to friends as well as to our neighbor upstairs, Felicia White and her two daughters. I was going back to Maine. I had landed a job teaching French at my alma mater, St. Francis College with a contract of $7,500 a year. My wife and daughter were glad to be going back home and so was I. I would be close again to my parents and two sisters. Dr. Hennedy was the department chair, the department of Humanities. I had contacted him for the open position in the French studies and I was given a contract given the promise that I would get my Ph.D. degree in the near future. That meant I would have to work diligently and assiduously during my summer months. I had done some research continuing what I had already done for my course paper. I would have to locate the books that I needed which meant that I would have to return to the Rockefeller Library at Brown when I needed to. I did not lose time enjoying its seashore and beaches and the seafood restaurants. I spent most of my days working on the much needed information and reading the plays carefully for my doctoral thesis. I checked in at the library at Bowdoin College some twenty miles away. St. Francis did not have the materials I needed. I did not go to Bates College in Lewiston neither to Colby College in Waterville. I was going to stick with Brown's library since I had noted the location of the books I wanted since they could not be taken out. I decided to spend the weekend in Providence reading and taking notes. I had a friend, Nelson, who lived in Pawtucket who offered me a place to stay while I was at Brown doing my research. Besides, his mother was a fine cook. I went back to Providence and of course to Pawtucket several times. It was a long trip and the driving was at times tiring. I had to prepare for my three classes come late August. The entire work load was demanding but I survived the hard work and I knew that in the end it would be worthwhile. Never in my life would I have even thought of getting a Ph.D. I kept telling myself that it was beyond my financial means and my intellectual capacity. But when the opportunity presented itself, I grabbed it and willed myself to succeed because it was in me and I had willed it that way. It was my drive to get an education with an advanced degree at a prestigious institution. It's not that I was proud and snobbish, haughty and climbing up the social ladder for the sake of prestige. I simply wanted to obtain an education, and go as far as the doctorate once I had been driven to it, then get a teaching job at a college and earn a decent living while enjoying my intellectual career as a teacher. I did not want to spend my life in a shoe shop or a mill doing menial work that had no meaning to it. I wanted more than a job. I wanted a career that would guarantee me intellectual challenges and opportunities to grow and blossom forth as a person and as a teacher. French has a word *épanouir* that fits exactly what I mean, to blossom, to open up.

Prior to even begin working on my dissertation, I had to take what is called prelims. Preliminary exams are required before a graduate student is allowed to begin work on a doctoral dissertation. Mine covered the entire span of French studies: the Middle Ages, the Renaissance, the Classical Age, the Romantic period and the 20th Century literature. I was told that the department would select two areas on which I would be tested but I would not find out before the exams. So, I had to study all of them in order to be prepared for whatever Century was being given to me the prelims. I was truly nervous about such an exam but I tried to be relaxed about it. I had taken all the required courses and I felt prepared for the two days of the prelims. When I got the two questions they were on the Middle Ages and the Classical period. I wrote some four blue books on each one. I did it in two full days of thinking and writing. I got out of there exhausted but content that I had done well. My right hand felt cramped from writing. I was to hear about the results in a few days. I do not exactly remember how I was informed about the results but I do remember getting a postcard from the registrar's office that it was official, I was a candidate to the doctorate in French studies. I kept that card for years until I decided that it was not necessary to hold on to it. I told myself after the prelims, another hurdle done. Now, I have to write the dissertation. No small matter.

I never thought that writing a doctoral dissertation would be that lengthy nor, at times grievous on both time and human energy. The worse part was receiving the final comment from my advisor that he was retiring and was giving up his role as dissertation advisor. He also let me know that he did not think I was doing very well with my writing and that he was awaiting for my ending with a worthwhile conclusion. He did not seem to think that I had brought my statements about Corneille's plays to a convincing effort to pull all of the strings together, as he put it. So, I was left without an advisor. I was called in the department chair office which was now being held by temporary chair. He was a Frenchman and appeared to me as a haughty and supercilious man. After a few words about the dissertation, he asked me how important was the dissertation to me and how important was getting my doctoral degree. I was flabbergasted. I did not know what to answer. I was speechless. All I could say was that it was most important to finish my dissertation and get my degree. I wanted to retain my teaching position at St. Francis College. I left him there without too many words of encouragement on his part. Fortunately, Professor Kuhn returned as chair and we had a good conversation about the lack of professionalism on the part of the French temporary chair and his lack of sensitivity to my situation as ABD[all but dissertation]. I thought he was telling me obliquely that the Frenchman was an ass. He then assured me that another advisor would be appointed and that I should not worry too much about my candidacy for the Ph.D. I remained in good standing and that meant that he trusted me and my academic skills.

That is when Professor Beverly R. became my advisor, the one I said that I would never want to work with. Life, academic life is filled with irony.

I had decided early on to write both my master's thesis and my doctoral dissertation in French. I figured that since this was a French program of studies I was going to write in French. I did not realize that the rules established by the department allowed only native speakers such as the French, the Québécois, the Swiss et al. to do so. I told myself that they did not realize the importance of Francophone heritage and language were to my ethnic group, the Franco-Americans. No one prevented me from writing in French and so I persisted in my decision to write my thesis and the dissertation in French. I was on a roll. I was going to show everyone that I wasn't a canuck nor a damn boot-licking student with no amount of both self-pride and *fierté*. I had learned to take my stand when the time came to claim my rights as a Franco-American. I think the French Studies faculty respected me for that.

After much research, reading and contemplating on what and how I was going to write my dissertation, I put together a plan or should I say a proposal that included fourteen plays from 1633 to 1651, the most fecund period of Corneille's career as a playwright. I was going to explore the important word and notion of *bas/bassesse* followed by synonyms such as *indigne, infâme, lâche*. Then I was to analyze the characters associated with the notion of *bassesse*. Finally, I was going to include a repertory of the term *bassesse* and its synonyms and reveal how many times these words had been used in a given play. I spent a lot of time doing just that. Finally, I would draw a conclusion at the end of my study and that was a crucial factor in my dissertation. It was expected from every reader of the dissertation, especially my advisor.

I started writing in the summer of 1969 while I was preparing for the classes I was going to teach in the fall. Needless to say I was enthused by my work both as an ABD and a novice teacher. The first draft that I sent my advisor was returned to me with loads of comments and questions written in red ink.

I was perturbed and astounded at the many questions raised by my advisor. Questions that I so often had a hard time answering. I came to a point when I thought he was giving me a hard time and that he was trying to berate me for my ideas and my writing. Would he ever be pleased with me is the question I posed to myself. After several drafts I sent my advisor, I received the last draft with so much red ink that I thought he would never accept my dissertation. I told my wife that I was fed up with his negative comments. I was going to throw the whole damn thing in the fire and forget about the dissertation. However, I got over it and continued the editing, corrections and whatever had been sent to me. I was determined not to give up. Finally, my advisor wrote to me telling me that he was accepting the dissertation and that he was going to pass the direction of the dissertation over to another professor since he was going on leave to Paris. The professor was Henry M. and I was relieved immensely.

What needed to be done at this juncture was the typing. I got in touch with a secretary at St. Francis, Rita S., and asked her to do it. She was a professional typist. She accepted and began the project. I had a deadline to meet. If not done on time I would have to pay an extra fee and the award of the degree would be delayed. The typist then informed me that it was taking much time to type since it was in French and she had to deal with accents. I told her to forget the accents and that I was going to put them in manually. She had the task done in less than a week. I rushed to get it signed and officially approved. It was signed by the advisor for of the dissertation, Beverly R. and by two readers, one in the French department and the other by a professor outside of the French studies, One was a woman, Laura D. whom I saw before going to class once and the other John E. whom I never met in person.

Following the submission of my dissertation there was the defense, the last step of the process. I was to defend it in front of several members of the French department. That made me very nervous. In the meantime, I was informed that my advisor would not be there since he would be away on leave. Professor Henry M. would replace him. What a godsend, I told myself. I liked Professor Henry M. for he was kind and generous as well as he had a super personality. He was easy to talk to. Before actually sitting down for the defense, he and I had a long chat about the procedures and dissertation itself. He told me to be frank and transparent about the entire matter and that I was the author of the dissertation and I knew best about it. That if I could not respond to some of the questions, I should simply say, I do not know. I was afraid that some older professor would quiz me intently and make me feel ignorant and unsure about the quality of the dissertation.

When I walked into the room where I was to defend my work, I felt extremely nervous. My hands were cold and I was trembling. However, when I began answering the first question, I relaxed and felt that I was master of my work and I answered the question intelligently and coherently. At one point, I was even able to cite the exact page number I was referring to. Everything was going smoothly until the 20th Century literature professor started asking questions about contemporary plays I had never read. It appeared to me that he was trying to impress the senior members of the department. I could see that some professors didn't seem to understand the intent of his questions. I felt the same way. So, I started asking him questions presuming I would test his weaknesses in classical theater. I was the challenger and no longer the unknowing defender. That gave a pause to the entire defense and the chair stopped the young fearless professor in his tracks. I sighed contentedly relieved that I had overcome the strain of contention. We all left the room each one smiling and chatting and congratulating me. I knew I had succeeded in defending my dissertation. I was gloriously accepted into their rank as a proven Ph.D. My pro-tem advisor shook my hand and warmly congratulated me inviting me to lunch. I felt free at last, free of the demands of French graduate studies and the awesome requirements of the program. It was as if I had gone through the martyrdom of words, rules and ideas. All I had to do was wait until commencement for my degree. I had saved up dollar by dollar every week to buy my cap and gown and I could not wait to wear them officially with merit and pride. It would be my badge of honor that I had worked so hard to get for my peers at St. Francis even the president had been pestering me when I was going to get my degree. I did get it in early June 1975. That was the apogee of my formal education. What began as my planned desire for an education blossomed into a reality that would last beyond my retirement. It was truly worthwhile because it opened so many doors and so many opportunities that I would not have had without a formal education. I began ten years later than most students who start after high school but I caught up with them. I was twenty-eight years old when I started my undergraduate studies. I never in my life expected to go to graduate school culminating in the doctorate. There were certainly hurdles to jump but I managed to jump with determination and prowess. The prowess of a convinced and valiant knight on his quest for success. Oddly enough, the mascot for St. Francis students was the knight.

Some of the doors that were opened to me were the opportunities to travel abroad. Of course there were possibilities to get to Quebec City and to Montreal. All I had to do was to travel by car. I first went to Quebec on a grant. I went with a fellow professor Robert P. and a teacher from St. Dom's High School in Lewiston, Maine. Our French department had written a grant sponsored by the Quebec Government's cultural ministry and we had received $20,000 for out project. It consisted of an educational cooperation between college and high school. It was entitled, French-Canadian Culture and Literature Course that proposed to educate and sensitize senior-level students to their own heritage and appreciate French-Canadian literature. The proposal was put together in 1972-73 by Hervé Poissant, the coordinator of the proposed program. Sister Solange o.s.u was the senior year teacher who taught French and French culture that included French-Canadian history and culture at St.Dom's High School, Lewiston, Maine. She had received her master's degree from Laval University with a concentration in that field. Students would receive four college credits for the course she was teaching. Most of her students were French-speaking and did very well in that particular endeavor. Part of the grant was used to develop pedagogical and cultural materials. I was involved with the program and visited Sister's classroom at least one a month and discussed what the students were doing as well as answering students' questions. One component of the program was a visit to Quebec. The travel was planned for the middle of March during the spring break. We all stayed at the Ursuline convent in Ancienne-Lorette, a few miles away from Quebec City. We visited several sites as well as attended a play at the Grand Théâtre du Québec. The offering for that week was "Charbonneau et le Chef". It was a play based on the struggles and rivalry of Monseigneur Charbonneau archbishop of Montreal and Quebec Prime Minister, Maurice Duplessis. It dealt with the strike in Asbestos, Quebec of 1949. It was a spectacular play well delivered by consummate artists. I truly enjoyed the performances every actor gave. The play enjoyed a fantastic success in Quebec with 163 performances in Quebec alone and 91 on tour. The company estimated 264,200 spectators in all. Whenever I had the chance to return to Quebec, I tried to go and see a play at the Grand Théâtre. I was never disappointed. Sister Solange also put on several student plays such as *Tit-Coq* by Gratien Gélinas, *Le Temps des*

Lilas and *Un Simple Soldat* by Marcel Dubé. They were all well received by the general public who faithfully attended each year. This program introduced me not only to Quebec but to its cultural richness specifically its literature. My graduate studies in French at Brown had not included this literature.

Then came other academic avenues such as invitations to workshops, panel discussions, visits to Laval University in Quebec, and participation in projects at the Franco-American Center at the University of Maine. I continued teaching in the Foreign Language department at St. Francis College. I developed new courses in French literature as well as humanities offerings that included team-teaching. The department was no longer a department on its own but it became part of the Humanities Department that included English, Philosophy, Theology, Political Science, Mathematics, History, Fine Arts, and languages. I would eventually become its chair. This was the result of the diminishing importance of the humanities in the curriculum. The college tried to survive as an institution by introducing more practical approaches such as Physical Therapy and Occupational Therapy as well as nursing. Eventually, the rise of health care interests came to peak when the college added an osteopathic medical school and the institution became the University of New England. Foreign languages were no longer a requirement and French became an elective that few students took. I was given a terminal contract. My academic future looked grim. There were few if none teaching position out there. I applied to several universities such as Vanderbilt. Vanderbilt told me that I was overly qualified for a position in French they had advertised. Finally I was offered the job of registrar and immediately took it with the understanding that I would be able to teach one course per semester voluntarily without remuneration. I so wanted to remain in teaching. The job of registrar lasted until I was offered to become chair of the humanities upon the recommendation of the political science professor who was leaving for another job in New Mexico. I thank Frank P. for giving me the chance to have a full-time position in the humanities. I had six teachers under me as well as several adjunct professors that I hired to teach courses that we no longer staffed with full-time teachers such as in the fine arts and theology. I had my full responsibilities as chair plus that of teaching two courses per semester. That was indeed a heavy academic load but I enjoyed it and gave it my all.

I was about that time that decided that I wanted to write and get published. I was an associate professor and I then qualified for the rank of full professor since I had put in my time. I wrote a self-evaluation and attached it to a formal request for promotion. It eventually went to the dean and to a promotion committee for recommendation. After two months, I was told that I was being promoted to full professor. I considered that another rung in my ladder of success. I loved keeping busy in my academic endeavors and I looked forward to my first novel. In the meantime I met a social worker, Jacques who told me of meeting an old wood carver who did all kinds of woodcarvings. He and his wife, Eva, lived Biddeford. They had emigrated to the States where he first worked as a blacksmith. Most of their lives were spent on a farm in Saco, Maine. The old farmer/blacksmith had given up dealing with horseshoes and other metal work because people no longer travelled by horse buggies. They owned a car. He had decided upon retirement to do wood sculptures. Many of them were designed from his own experience as a blacksmith. He added metal parts to some of his carvings such as the tip cart that he did. They were all folk sculptures in wood and metal that reflected his many years as a farmer and blacksmith. I loved all of his work. I deemed them to be works of folk art and worthy of public display. Eventually, I organized a display at the college and invited him and his wife to take a look at the entire display in our library. His wife told me later that her husband had never expected to have his work in public display and that he was ever so pleased with it. I then decided to write a book about Adelard Coté's work. That was his name. I gathered all the information I would need from his wife. I next asked my neighbor Stephen Muskie, a professional photographer, to take photos of the man, his wife, their home and, of course, Adelard's sculptures. We had received a small grant from the Department of Education Title VII through the National Materials for French and Portuguese Development Center in Bedford, New Hampshire. It was a well-documented and well-illustrated book on a local folk artist. It had a bilingual text, French and English. I included a short history of Biddeford and Saco. I gave the study the title *L'Enclume et le couteau/*

The Life and Work of Adelard Coté, folk artist. This was my very first publication and I was indeed proud of it.

I had decided to write some kind of memoir that the publisher eventually called *roman-vérité*, a real-life novel. I gave it the title of *Le Petit Mangeur de Coeur-Saignants*, (The Little Eater of Bleeding Hearts). I took that from the story my mother had related to me about my eating actual flowers, the bleeding hearts that my great aunt, Elizabeth Simard, had next to her porch. I was about one and a half years old then. That became the metaphor for the young lad eating his esthetics. In the meantime, I was writing another novel based on my maternal mother's life as an immigrant to the States and my mother's life as I had witnessed it. Originally, I had wanted to write a saga of the Franco-Americans that would have the title of *Au Fil de L'Eau*, as the water flows, since mills were often located next to rivers and most Francos worked in mills in New England. Since most of the story dealt with two women, mother and daughter, I decided to change the entire thrust of the intended saga. The saga would have been too much of an effort on my part to include generations upon generations of immigrants to New England. So I decided to focus on my mother's and her mother's life and call it *Deux Femmes, Deux Rêves*.

I still had not submitted my first writing to a publisher since it had to be a publisher of French works and I did not know any. Upon the recommendation of a friend from the ethnic history department of Laval University, Jean Simard, I submitted my second work to a publisher called Les Éditions de Mortagne in a town next to Montreal called Boucherville. Jean had just published his very important and impressive work on the religious art of Quebec, *Les arts sacrés au Québec* in 1989. Based on his recommendation I submitted the manuscript of my novel *Deux Femmes, Deux Rêves*. A few weeks later, I received a call from the coordinator of publications at Mortagne asking me to meet with him to discuss my manuscript. I leaped for joy at this news. I went to his office and he showed me the stack of manuscripts and he told me that he received hundreds of them in a month's time. He decided to select some for publication once he had read the first two or three lines. I sat there stunned. He then told me at lunch that he had selected my novel since he found it very interesting and saleable once in print. He had to discuss the matter with his boss. I returned home thinking that it was a closed deal. However, I later learned that the coordinator had been let go due to some bad sales with books he had highly recommended for publication. The matter of the publication of my manuscript was now entirely in the hands of the owner-publisher's brother. He assured me by phone that the publication of my work was guaranteed. Several weeks passed and I had not heard a word from Les Éditions de Mortagne. When I did reach the publishing company I was told that the owner/publisher, Monsieur Permingeat, refused to publish my work. He simply did not like novels. He thought they were not profitable items for him and his company. I was shocked and practically in tears. I was so very much disappointed. That was my first failed trial at getting published. It would not be the last one.

Later on, I met a nun who lived in Chicoutimi, Quebec, Sister Béa, who offered to submit the manuscript of my first work to a publisher in her city. The publisher was JCL (Jean-Claude Larouche). To my great joy and appreciation, the work was accepted for publication. I finally had my second book published, a novel in French.

CHAPTER FOUR

Teaching and travel

Teaching is also a learning experience. When I was in Providence attending graduate school at Brown University, I was asked by my daughter's elementary school to replace a French teacher who was on leave. Not only was I actually going to use my academic skills but I had to learn the skills of pedagogy, the art and science of teaching. I had never formally taught before except to give a workshop or two. Unfortunately, I came up with disciplinary problems with one of the students, Charlie was his name, who kept interrupting me in class. I told the principal about it and she reprimanded the student and told him that he was wasting not only precious time but also the value of dollars and cents. One day I had him sit in front of all the students thinking that would subdue him if not humiliate him a bit, but he enjoyed the glow of being at the very center of the life of the class. When an interruption occurred he would say out loud, "Woops, there goes a nickel, there goes a dime." I was giving him center stage and I felt outdone by this comic of a young student. I stopped my volunteer teaching at Holy Family School telling the principal I was too busy to teach her fifth grade. Actually I wanted to teach but I could not stand Charlie and others who made me feel uncomfortable. My hands and forehead were sweating so uneasy was I standing there not knowing what to do. How can one establish discipline in class, I wondered. Fortunately, I did not encounter any Charlies at the college level. But there was the problem of motivation when it came time for assigned readings and oral reports. I never overcame that. I was especially troubled when I taught a literature class and some students came to class unprepared. How can a teacher have a discussion in class if students don't do the readings, is a question I often asked myself. If students didn't like a teacher lecturing and delivering a long presentation of notes that often bored many a student, how could he begin a discussion if students had not read the prescribed reading, was evident to me. I could never figure that out. I discovered later on that the problem was that some students had a reading capacity of the fifth or sixth grade level. How could they have graduated from high school, I wondered. This question would linger in my mind right through my teaching experience until I retired.

At St. Francis College, we faculty members were given the choice and freedom to be creative in our choice of courses being offered. I was free to create courses that were not particularly about French since I followed the broader humanities guidelines. We did not have a major in French anymore. I tried to be practical in my pursuit of courses being offered as electives as well as courses that met the broader requirements of the Humanities Department such as a team-taught course on Western Civilization or World Religions as well as World History and Literature. Most team-taught courses consisted of two faculty members. I chose to teach World History and Literature with an Education teacher who loved the humanities. She was an adjunct professor named Dottie. She was well versed in history and I could tell she loved literature including philosophy and religion. She was an excellent match for me. We had the same pedagogical views and we put a course perspective together that was varied and interestingly educational. The readings were books and articles that both of us favored due to our familiarity with them and our desire to share our views and insights. One of the courses was called "The Enlightened Philosopher and the Religious Dimension of Thinkers." I was able to include one of my favorite works of literature, "Frankenstein" by Mary Shelley that I treasured. It had so many dimensions including the act of creation, the monster idea, and playing God as well as being human in a society that often seeks dehumanization. Teaching literature with dimensions of history, philosophy and theology was a true academic challenge for me since I loved reading and research that enlightened me and offered me fodder for my teaching. I felt that I was not being restricted to one subject matter like French. Of course, I still offered some French courses when needed but they were few and far apart. That's when I turned to translations so that students could learn about some of the classic literature of the Francophone world such as "*La Chanson de Roland,*" "*Madame Bovary*", "*Maria Chapdeleine*" and poetry by Léopold Léopold Sédar Senghor from Africa who became a member of *L'Académie Française.* He was a major proponent of the concept of *Négritude.* I met him once in Vermont after asking him a question about negritude and its impact on literature and he told his consorts that this was one of the best questions asked during his presentation/discussion. This led me to include the concept of negritude in my teaching about Francophone culture and literature. The idea of *la Francophonie*, French speaking, writing and belonging outside France, meant that I was part of it as a Franco-American. My ethnic group was attached to that of Haiti, the French-speaking Caribbean Isles, and the French-speaking Canadians as well as several others meant that I belonged to a large number of Francophones. I had an identity. I was part of something, a cultural community of French-speaking people.

My teaching gave me the opportunity of challenging myself and plunging into more universal concepts and visions of links not only to the past but to the future of fast developing world of literature, the arts both visual and performing. Teaching for me meant growing into maturity with an expansive view of education. I was being educated as well as the students that I taught. Furthermore, travel became a very important component of my teaching. Travel meant broadening my horizons and capturing the essence of cultural experiences. I was going to take every possibility of travel offered to me. Whenever I could, I would include students in my travels.

My first academic venture in France was offered to me by the French Consulate in Boston in 1979. It was sponsoring a three-week workshop in Marly-le-Roi as part of the 10th Annual Summer Institute at the *Institut National d'Éducation Populaire* . I did not realize then that it was being offered all over the world to French-speaking people. All I had to do was pay the airfare. It was my first time going to France by myself. I was very nervous. It was my very first overseas flight on Air-France. What would be the first moves I would make once out of the plane. Where would I go for the first night. A friend of mine had told me about a cheap hotel, l'Hôtel de la Tulippe. I took a taxi from the airport Charles de Gaulle and told the cab driver to bring me to that hotel. It was mid-afternoon. I was to go to my destination the following morning. I got a room for eight francs. It was a very small room with no bathroom. I would have to go down the hallway to find a common one. As it got dark out, I began to be scared. I felt like a foreigner. The following morning, I got up early and went out for a coffee and a croissant. All along, I wondered if the Parisians would understand my French since I was not one of them. I came from far away and I was a Franco-American. Well, they all did, the hotel manager, the server at the lunch wagon, and the taxi driver. Now, I had to go to the train station, la Gare Saint-Lazare and get a ticket for Marly-le-Roi. Dealing with francs was not difficult once I had gotten familiar with them. I then took my luggage and entered the second class *non fumeur* car and took a seat. When we arrived at Marly-le-Roi, I simply followed the crowd that I presumed was headed to the workshop area. I managed very well for the registration and was given a private room in a student dormitory. It was clean and very modern. I was greatly relieved for my fears of getting lost in a territory unknown to me were dissipated now that I was comfortable with my French and my ability to converse with other participants. There were people from Syria, Belgium, Greece and Nova Scotia as well as other countries. We had the choice of three different workshops. I chose the one with a French-speaking English artist by the name of Kyle M. who was going to teach the group visual arts by means of posters. It got to be a very interesting workshop that taught me unusual skills in print-making. One of the posters that I worked on was the enlarged human eye with radiating photos of the workshop participants. I still have that poster. I made friends with people from Syria and other Arab countries. They were all curious and enthused about my being an American. I was one of two Americans there. The other one came from Louisiana. By mid-week, we were given a full-day break and most of the participants went to Paris. My first venture in Paris. Paris that I had so desired to see. It was part of my adventures that I was going to share with my students once I got home.

It was at that time that I met a man from Lebanon named Zaki Chokor. He was a tall, dashing and remarkable man with piercing dark eyes and with a smile that could light up an entire room. I had never met a Muslim before and I found him to be deeply religious and loyal to his faith. I got to become friends with him and I considered him to be an extraordinary person with a song in his heart and on his lips. Once at table, he opened up with a song with delight that revealed his exuberance and joy at being together with people he recognized as friends. I thought to myself that I was always taught not to sing aloud at table for that meant that I would cry later on. That was one of our ethnic folk beliefs. But, it was a real joy to hear Zaki sing out loud with a charming tenor voice at table that noontime. Evidently the reluctance of singing at table was not one of his concerns but rather it was an acceptable way of proclaiming one's joy. I admired that and it was an impressive mark of *joie de vivre* at that moment for me.

Once all workshops were terminated, we had a marvelous reception with wine and Viennese pastries. These were excellent and delightful. I gorged myself on these delicacies. Everyone sang and wished each other farewell. Every participant, it seems, was reluctant in leaving people they had met and enjoyed. I certainly did. The following day, most participants went their way. Some went home, Zaki stayed on at Marly-le-Roi for another workshop and I went and stayed at the *Cité Internationale Universitaire de Paris* at the *Fondation Hellénique*. I had met a woman from Greece at the workshop and we became close friends. She is the one who suggested that I stay at the Greek house since I was looking for a place to stay for the rest of my journey in France. She had even informed a friend of hers at the *Fondation* to expect me. I was grateful for the contact. Some of the members there thought I was Greek.

I took the train back to Marly-le-Roi to visit Zaki before I returned home to the U.S. It was an enjoyable visit with someone I had learned to love as a close friend. I remembered one episode in our living at the students' quarters when Zaki had caught an awful cold and his lungs were congested. I had gone to pay him a visit and saw him lying in bed with a deep sense of anguish and a need to get help from someone. The lady from Syria offered him all kinds of medication that she had brought with her from Syria but he refused her offer thinking it would be dangerous to take unknown medication. I offered to go to the pharmacy and get a decongestant. I returned to his room and rubbed the liniment or was it a cream, I don't remember, on his chest. He responded well to it. I remember that he was ever grateful for the care I gave him at a time when he felt alone being away from home. I was told later on that when someone is ill within the Muslim families, the entire family is there to take care of the patient. Good and tender care is of the highest priority. Zaki welcomed my being there as an adopted family member so-to-speak. That was a favorable act of friendship on my part as well as a memorable act of appreciation on Zaki's part.

As I was leaving the workshops location and going to take the train back to Paris, Zaki held my hand and I could see a tear falling down his right cheek. I was so touched by this that I felt like shedding a tear myself. I had a big lump in my throat. Apparently in the space of two and half weeks our friendship had blossomed into a binding closeness that I would never forget. When we saw the train at a distance, Zaki kissed my cheek and I felt I didn't really want to leave him. I stopped there in my tracks while the train left the local station. I knew I had to leave want to or not. Zaki urged me on and I reluctantly took the next train with a heavy heart. I never thought I would ever meet such a man, a man from faraway Lebanon who would so touch the fibers of my being. We corresponded for three months once I got home to my teaching job. Then I lost touch with him. I never heard from him again. I have considered this a loss due to the fact that losing a true friend like Zaki is indeed a loss, a hole in the heart. This may sound sentimental and nostalgic to some but I say that with genuine feelings and true intent. Zaki, I will never forget you, my friend, *mon ami de coeur.*

Over the years I went to Paris some thirty-four times whether by invitation or by desire to be there. Of those times, I went to Paris on two sabbaticals. After each seven years of teaching we are granted a sabbatical. I took half a year since I could not afford to lose half of my salary if I took a full year. My proposal was the study of the Francophone area of Quebec and New England compared to France. Prior to that I had gone to France in 1981 at the invitation of the French Consulate in Boston. It was a three-week study program on the methodology and localities of folklore. The Program was based at the *Musée d'Arts et Traditions Populaires* in Paris. Two other Franco-Americans accompanied me, Robert Perreault and Michelle Cotnoir, both from New Hampshire. We were to study the cultural similarities of Francophone New England and Normandy as well as Brittany. Brittany is the northern geographic teapot spout of France. It's a very colorful area on the Atlantic coast much like New England. It has its own customs and language, a dialect resembling that of the Celtic resonance. The local dialect is called *le Breton bretonnant* which means a Breton who speaks the dialect. We met a popular author whose autobiography, *Le Cheval d'orgueil* was written in this dialect then translated into French, English and other languages. It sold more than a million copies in France. I bought my copy and had it signed by Pierre-Jakes Hélias, the author. He was proud of meeting three Americans who spoke French. While in Brittany we visited several sights. We went to a movie location much used by cinematographers for historical films dealing with Medieval knights. We enjoyed the local food and delighted in the songs and dance of the people dressed in their costumes with the ladies sporting their colorful *coiffes*, the lace headdresses representing various regions of Brittany. I was in my element for I so enjoyed this trip and the many discoveries of colorful and exciting exploration of a part of France I had never seen before.

My first sabbatical occurred in the fall of 1993 and I was somewhat jittery about it. It was my first adventure in France for three whole months. I had rented an apartment through an agency in Paris. The apartment was on la rue de Chevreuse in the sixth arrondissement. It was owned by a woman who lived in Switzerland. It turned out to be a lovely and very clean studio apartment with a large bathroom, and a small kitchen area. It included a small table with chairs and a comfortable couch which opened up as a bed. There was a large window that opened up on rue Montparnasse the main avenue where shops and restaurants were attainable on foot. I was able to locate a small boulangerie in the back street where I would go purchase each morning a demi-baguette[a full one gets stale fast]. I also discovered a small grocery store not too far from where I lived. Almost every morning I had ham and eggs with slices of baguette and jam. Sometimes I had a fresh and flaky croissant. I cooked many a meal in my apartment. Meals at restaurants became too expensive for my budget. I much rather spend my money on books. When I needed groceries I also went to outdoors *marchés* right across from where I lived. What beautiful and splendid array of vegetables, fruits, cheeses, meats, and flowers as well as other varieties of edible and non-edible offerings. Every day, there was an open-air market somewhere in the city where people flocked. Sometimes, I went to the rue du Bac and stopped in at the chapel of the Miraculous Medal where Our Lady appeared to Saint Catherine Labouré whose incorrupt body lies under the altar on the right. It's a favored place of many a visitor coming from far away. On the corner of the street there is a large market called *Le Grand Marché* where I purchased some of my food. The variety and quality were superb. I never lacked choice food for my evening meal. As for lunch, I took a quick meal at a small restaurant at low prices anywhere I happened to be in my wandering around Paris. From early in the morning, I would begin my long walks starting at the Jardin du Luxembourg in my so-called back yard, reach the Boulevard Saint Michel, and take a look at Notre-Dame Cathedral looming at a short distance. At times, I would go and visit the church to say my prayers in front of the medieval statue of the Virgin Mary, *la Reine de Paris,* and then turn around to gaze at the two rose windows, one on the right and one on the left. I made sure that the sun was shining that day so that I could fully enjoy the splendor of the colored glass. The one I truly liked was the one on the right with a marvelous pinkish violet hue. I just stood there admiring the amazing craft of the medieval glaziers who had toiled with so much effort and skill. I was in awe of such marvelous art. I always felt that I was witnessing medieval history in stone and stained glass with the *arcs-boutants,* the flying buttresses, outside its gothic presence.

I especially loved to hop from stall to stall at the book vendors on the bridge crossing the Seine and treat myself to the delight of so many books and lithographs as well as old maps and prints of dress styles, *la mode* of different centuries. I often bought one of these for the Dean's secretary, Rena Deis, that I had befriended. She was like a southern belle,[she and her husband, Carl, had lived in the south of the U.S. several years] refined and a lover of art and periodic costumes. She had an entire collection of dresses and men's attire that she displayed at a yearly costume show. I loved pleasing her with my Paris offerings.

Of course, I would stop at various *pâtisseries* to gaze at the delightful pastries in the windows. So often would I go in and buy one for my evening meal. The clerks would always wrap it in a cone-shape container so as not to bruise the pastry. Such care and such artistic skill. Then I always looked forward to lunchtime, le *déjeuner,* when I would have an entire possibility of choice at my command and a reasonable price. No *Tour d'Argent or Le Café Vendôme* nor *La Closerie des Lilas* for me, especially no Ritz. The afternoon was spent in boutiques where books, embossed correspondence paper with matching envelopes, all sorts of printed cards and attractive calendars as well as splendid *bagatelles* that caught my eye were displayed. Then I would walk around trying to find Saint Sulpice, the church where Des Grieux and Manon meet surreptitiously and look for the boutique that sold *santons* those little painted clay "little saints"[that's the translation of the term] that are part of lovely *crèches* throughout France. They are made in Provence by such craftsmen as Carbonel. They're truly gems of the Christmas celebration. They come in different sizes. I started a collection right there in Paris and every time I went to Paris, I added to my collection. They're not cheap but well worth it. I now have some 72 pieces that I treasure and take out for display at Christmastime. Every visitor to my home during the holidays admire them and want to touch them. I warn them, "Ah! Ah1 Ah! Do not touch for the paint will stick to your fingers."

I enjoy *lèche-vitrine*[window-shopping] in Paris. There are so many tempting articles of clothing, expensive pens, colognes, perfumes for ladies, leather goods such as luggage and handbags, wallets made of very soft calf skin and snake skin, gloves as well as very expensive shoes made of crocodile skin tanned for luxury wear. All kinds of things for all kinds of people wanting to buy souvenirs from Paris. Something chic, something rare and something extraordinary that you cannot get home. I remember one year I bought a Cardin shirt for 75 francs in a *boutique de chemises,* they were tailored shirts and I did not even ask the price. Something from Paris. I once bought a pair of leather gloves. They were of a cinnamon color and they were very nice and I wore them for years until I lost them. Of course, everyone goes to the *Galerie Lafayette* where there are levels upon levels of choice products. And, there is la FNAC, a very large multi levels store where almost every single item of music can be found. I have spent many an hour there. I bought several CD albums of operas such as Manon and Tosca. So many people go shopping there like a flood of music seekers.

There are several *portes* in the metro system. These are the "doors" or exits one can take to go somewhere. There are also used as *correspondences*, meaning links from one *porte* to another as long as you do not get out of the metro. One that I always noticed was called Clignancourt. It was at the end of the entire span of *portes* on the list. Once you have mastered the metro routes you have at your disposal an easy travel method of transportation in Paris. I learned it quickly by following others and reading instructions. Well, one day I decided to go to Clignancourt specifically for the *Marché aux puces*, a very large flea market. I had read about it and decided to devote an entire day to walking in such a market. I left my apartment early in the morning and took the metro ending with the *Porte de Clignancourt*. I got off and followed the exiting crowd of people who were no doubt going to the flea market. When I got there, I was amazed at the vast extent of this market. As I walked from stall to stall, I realized that it was not just big but it was enormous. I could see all kinds of offerings such as clothes, jewelry, antique furniture, trinkets, pots and pans, scarves and headwear, remarkable items such as paper weights, and so many things I cannot all itemize here. It was indeed an adventure in shopping. I was amazed at what went on display here. One could spend an entire week looking and still not see everything. I bought a small yellow glass paper weight that I liked. I could not buy too large an item because I remembered that I would have to carry it in my luggage when I flew back home. One thing that caught my eye was a small doll. It looked as if it had been through a fire and was left with some vestiges of smoke and ashes. It looked cheap but nevertheless I wanted it. I was somehow charmed by this poor doll. It was made of some kind of pink celluloid and dressed in cheap thin black cotton pants with jacket, and some kind of a dull dark reddish bonnet on its head. The doll had moveable arms and legs with eyes that opened and closed. There was a yellowed sticker at the bottom of the jacket and it read, *A ceux qui me possèdent j'apporte le bonheur,* Whoever owns me I bring happiness. I loved it and what it said. Right away I thought this would make a good story what with the doll telling its story of where it had been all these years and who had owned it. It could be material for a fine novel, I told myself. Someday, I would write this story. Up to now, I have not written it but someday I will.

I remember going to the grand opera building built by Garnier, *l'Opéra de Paris.* I wanted to see the inside where so many people had been to see world-famous operas and where Maris Callas had sung to a loving audience. Her performance of "Norma" was outstanding and all of Paris applauded her singing for she had enthralled so many. As I climbed the *grand escalier,* I thought of the rich and famous who had been there such as Jaqueline Kennedy and Charles DeGaule. I did attend one opera, but I was seated in a box that was so hidden from the stage that I could hardly see anything. That was the only ticket I was able to get that day. Later, I would get to see the new opera house, *Opéra de Paris Bastille* a magnificent modern building with open seating. I had gone there to enjoy a performance of Offenbach's *Les Contes d'Hoffman.*

One of my cultural adventures was going to a small theater to see a play by Henry de Montherlant that I had read in college. It was a favorite of mine. *Le Cardinal d'Espagne* deals with Cardinal Cisneros and Jeanne la Folle, the Regent in Spain. The crazy one as they called her was not that insane. She could see things that others could not especially the proud and mighty cardinal who created tension between himself and Juana la Loca. It's a magnificent work of artistic drama. The theater was small but intimate. The actors were very good and gave a performance that was delightfully appealing. It rendered my reading of the play concrete and real.

Another delight for me was a performance by Nana Mouskouri at the well-known Olympia in Paris where may stars go when invited for a performance that attracts thousands of people. I decided one day to go to the Olympia and try to get a ticket for an upcoming performance by Nana Mouskouri. I was fortunate enough to get one at what I thought was a reasonable price. It was an evening performance. I left my apartment, took the metro and arrived at the Olympia in time to see the crowd waiting to get in. I had a seat in the second row up front. I could almost touch the singer who sang in so many languages. A young man sitting in front of me handed Nana a red rose whose thorns had been removed. She took it and handed it over to one of her assistants. I guessed that gesture of offering a thorn free rose was part of a ritual for a Mouskouri concert. The singing was marvelous and when she sang *Liberdad/Liberté* there was a great hush in the audience. I could tell that people were moved by this song that had become a favorite of not only Parisians but all over the world. I could have stayed there in the theater until the lights had been put out and the people had departed, but I knew I had to leave, take the metro and get back to my apartment. I had Nana Mouskouri's voice in my head all night even when I got up the next morning.

There are so many cultural possibilities in Paris such as theater, museums, opera, exhibits, concerts, ballet, libraries, talks and discussions and of course, cinema.

I discovered Marcel Pagnol and his great talent for putting into writing his own local history and culture, that of Provence. He was recognized for his great talent as a novelist, playwright and filmmaker when he was elected to *l'Académie Française* in 1946, the first filmmaker to become a member of this honored group. He is well known for the characters of Marius, César and Fanny. I went to see two films based on two his works, *Jean de Florette* and *Manon des Sources*. They were directed by the well-admired director Claude Berri. Featured in these two films are Yves Montand as "Papet", Daniel Auteuil as Ugolin and Gérard Dépardieu as Jean de Florette. Wonderful performances by these actors. The central theme is the essential value and need of water for people living in hot and dry Provence. The second part deals with Jean's daughter all grown up who discovers the treachery of "Papet" and Ugolin and plugs the source of the town water supply in her revenge. I so loved the films that I bought the novels and brought them home to read. I thought of using them in a proposed course that I never taught since I did not have the opportunity to teach a French literature course anymore.

Another film directed by Claude Berri, that I saw while in Paris was part of Zola's naturalist novel, *roman fleuve. Rougon-Macquart*. It's about miners and it's called, "Germinal". I liked this novel about *Étienne Lantier*, a kind of a rebel who is the victim of the system of economics gone haywire with the greed of investors and big money. It's a powerful drama of hard labor, sweat and tears, as well as dire poverty. Zola did much research on the plight of the coal miners in northern France. This novel is considered his masterpiece. I used it in one of my literature courses in translation. It was part of a selection of three novels that featured the hero as savior, *Étienne Lantier, Jean Valjean* of *Les Misérables* and Tom Joad of "The Grapes of Wrath". All three as the solitary heroes as I called them in my course.

I went to museums also. There was the grand Louvre where you can walk for days where you still could not take in each and every painting and sculpture so vast was the entire collection. I especially liked David's colossal painting *Le Sacre de Napoléon* with its exquisite realism. Why you can almost see the very fine rendering of the hairs of Napoleon's ermine. Then the museum of the Impressionists, le Musée d'Orsay, the former train station, where I spent hours looking at great paintings that have delighted art lovers for years. I loved this museum with its huge clock preserved from the train station of old. Then there was the Rodin Museum on rue Varenne. I admired "The Gates of Hell", "The Thinker" that everyone recognizes and several other sculptures. The one that I liked very much was "The Burghers of Calais", commissioned by the city of Calais. It's an historical aperçu as well as a marvelously sculpted piece that represents the six men who were to be executed until there was a reprieve. It's a stunning sculpture rendering the emotions of the condemned burghers.

The Musée de l'Orangerie houses Monet's "Waterlilies" and you can sit for a long time admiring the circular masterpiece like two of my older students did when I took a small group during one Winter Term. I went to Giverny twice and visited Monet's house and gardens as well as the pond of waterlilies and the bridge over which hangs the splendid wisterias. I took many photos there and almost fell into the pond so very close did I get to the water. The second time I went, I was greatly disappointed in that the whole place had been what I would call "marketized". You had to first go through the shop in order to go into the house and gardens. I felt totally disenchanted with the commercial changes.

As for the Centre Pompidou, the museum with its insides out, it seemed strange to me that such architecture stood there in the middle of Paris, the city of beauty and splendid creativity. But I suppose that anything goes with Paris as long as it's funded by someone or some agency. People flock to it and enjoy its modern offerings. I did not like any of the so-called works of art there. There was one painting that showed simply a streak of paint right down the middle. Is this art? I asked myself. I've seen some children's paintings that were so much better than this. Another instance was the metal locker painted green standing next to the escalator. I told my friend, Jean, a Québécois, that I could not see that object as art. Lockers are lockers with no esthetic sense. He replied that very often a so-called *objet d'art* is purchased by some *fonctionnaire* who insists that it's truly art and has it placed in a museum because he has control over some fund destined for art purchase. His taste on art is thus imposed on everyone, to all who visit the museum. I agreed with my friend on his assessment why the green locker was standing there in the Pompidou center. I suppose that such objects are considered art only because the esthetics on art objects has changed only because tastes have changed and oftentimes some tastes are weird if not tasteless. Should I accept the "green locker" as *un objet d'art* when my sense of esthetics refuses to do so? My sense of esthetics has been formed and culturally modified by years of learning from the masters and years of experience in contemplating art on exhibit. So, I think that I have a right to object when I think I should do so. That's what I tell my students when I teach a course on art and literature.

I must not forget the one time I was invited to go to Paris to a writers' conference dealing with international authors of French. It was under the sponsorship of the French Ministry, Francophone section with Alain Decaux as Minister. *Les États Généraux de la Création Francophone* was the title of the conference. I went there with my friend, Robert Perreault and we had a lavish reception with the choicest wines and a most delightful meal the second night we were there. It seemed truly a high class venue with government brass and famous people who attended. I met the Acadian author, Antonine Maillet and she told us that she was proud of the small delegation of Canadian and American Francophones. One of the highlights of the trip was my invitation to go and visit l'Académie Française where the famous 40, *les 40 Immortels*, sit and deliberate on the "*pureté de la langue*"(purity of the French language),and other important matters. The Academy was created by the illustrious Cardinal Richelieu in the 17th Century. I got to sit in one of the *sièges*/seats of the members. I told myself then that here is an unknown and not too famous an author sitting here. A poor little Franco-American like me sitting at l'Académie Française in Paris. Wow! It was a rare treat for me. I will never forget this. I was treated like royalty or somebody famous by the French ministry of cultural affairs who had invited me and I relished it.

I must add that the goal of the Academy was always to "purify" the French language of all regional words. However, the Academy later changed its rules and started admitting regional words and terms such as *la brunante* and *achaler*, dusk and to bother continually. Maurice Druon, the Perpetual Secretary of the Academy had put together a dossier entitled, *Mots de la Francophonie Retenus Par l'Académie Française*, 1989. I was given a copy listing many regional words including several French-Canadian/Franco-American expressions that were considered what I would call "outlaw" words that were prohibited in the standard usage of French when I was growing up. I simply smiled and told myself that "our" language had finally been accepted by the high court of words in Paris. That made me proud as an author who uses words to produce novels and articles. Proud to be a Franco-American.

I must add to all of this are my trips to Mexico. I went there several times during our January Winter Terms. However, one very important one was the trip in January—February 2000. I had been doing research for my Transcultural Health Care course. The Dean of our Osteopathic Medical School had encouraged me to consider this cultural dimension of the humanities. So I went to Cuernavaca, Mexico to establish professional contacts for our medical school in view of establishing fourth year clerkships that would offer students cultural latino-Mexican perspectives with holistic healing. I established a significant contact with the *Institudo Nacional de Salud Publico* and a School of Public Health Professor and researcher in alternative medicine. This whole new dimension of the humanities helped me to become cognizant of the range of health care and cultural traditions. I must say that I never missed an opportunity to broaden my own academic and cultural horizons since I truly appreciated learning and teaching.

CHAPTER FIVE

Brazil

At this point I want to talk about Brazil. Yes, that faraway country where their summers are our winters and their winters are our summers. I went there after our university was apprised that we did not receive the Fulbright Hays Grant. It took much research and a lot of forms and writing on the part of our grant writing department to submit our application. The office in Washington told us to re-apply. We did that the following year. In the meantime, a dozen of us faculty members who had applied for the unique opportunity to spend three weeks in Brazil had studied Portuguese under the tutorship of a lovely dark-eyed Brazilian woman named Wilma Sampaio de Oliveira who came to teach us the language in preparation for our grant. I learned quite a bit with her since Portuguese has similarities with Spanish and French, all three being romance languages.

When it was found out that we did not receive the grant, a good friend of mine, Sister Priscille Roy, a Good Shepherd nun who was spending time in Brazil as a missionary and happened to be in her convent in Biddeford, contacted me to discuss the situation with Brazil. She told me that since I had spent weeks preparing for the Brazil trip, she offered me an opportunity to go to her convent in Brazil and spend some time with her people, the students and the displaced and orphaned people who were under her wings and had sought shelter at Bom Pastor, the residence. It did not take me long to accept her offer. Besides, I was on vacation. I did not have to teach during the summer months. All I had to do was to purchase an airline ticket. I dug into my pockets and came up with the necessary money. Once there, I would be lodged and fed by Irma Priscilla and her convent. I brought enough money to pay for others expenses. I had to fly to Miami then on to Natal in Brazil where someone was to meet me at the airport. Here I was off to another continent alone and trusting in the Good Lord to guide me and protect me from any harm such as robbers and no-do-gooders. I was really taking a chance since I knew no one in Brazil except for Irma Priscilla. But, she was at least seventy miles away from Recife. She was going to pick me up three days after my arrival. In the meantime, I was going to stay at the Jesuit House in Recife. I was told that there was a Jesuit there from California who spoke English. Unfortunately, he was not there since he was away for some excursion. He would not return for a couple of weeks. I managed with the little Portuguese that I had under my belt. Fortunately, the superior spoke English and invited me, one day, to accompany him on a tour of the area. I was delighted. His name was Theodoro Paolo Severino Peters. He was a tall, handsome well-educated man and he knew both the geography and culture of the Brazilians especially those who live in the northern part. Brazil is a vast country in territory and its people. I was willing to learn whatever he offered me along with the experience of being and living there.

I saw some painted figurines called folklore pieces that came as collections on a clay plate. I got three plates with each one having a theme or representation of some folklore characters. All the figures are tiny and well created. I have one that represents dancers, *Bumba meu boi dança de carnival de Olinda*. I find them exquisite. I so desired to get them but I did not have the money on me. He offered me to pay for them and that I would be able to pay him back once back at the house. I thought it was so kind of him. I believe he realized that I was a teacher and that I collected folk art. Two days later, Sister Priscilla arrived at the Jesuit House in Recife bringing with her two other nuns who were to depart for the U.S. and Canada the following day. Mid-afternoon of the day of her arrival, I got into her jeep and off we went to Bom Pastor, her residence. She was a damn good driver and she knew the territory. Of course she had been in Brazil some 18 years. She had learned the language on her own and made friends easily. She told me that she always wanted to live in a country where there was plenty of sunshine and it's warm year round. When the chance to go to Brazil came her way, she immediately took it.

Sister Priscille took good and loving care of children in need and of women who were abandoned, neglected or on drugs and alcohol. She took them in, housed them for a while and tried to rehabilitate them the best she could. She sent them back into the local community with some money in their pockets. She also gave them some fruits to sell because she did not want to give them too much pocket money since she knew that they would spend it within a day or two and return to their ways of depravity and loneliness. She gave them something to sell so that they would learn to support themselves. She had one young woman, Immaculata, who always returned later a week or two she realized she had no more resources and could not survive being pregnant with child. She had had several pregnancies before and giving her babies up for adoption and relying on the religious community to salvage her tenuous life.

The last I heard was good news, said Sister Priscille. Immaculata had decided to keep her last child and continue living at Bom Pastor.

One day, Sister Priscille drove me and another nun to Jardim de Piranhas some fifty miles away. We had to go through the *sertaõ* a stretch of desert, before getting to the mission. I did not get to see those deadly fish the piranhas but I saw the waters where they abound. The sisters had a few missions around Bom Pastor. They tried to teach, support and evangelize the natives, especially the poor. They even had a summer camp for children. It was more of a shack on a lake but it suited the children who could not afford to go to the beach near the ocean. The all came from the poor and jobless side of the tracks. Many of them lived in poverty and barely eked out an existence by selling fruits and objects they fabricated. Children could not really attend school although schooling was free, paid for by the government. Except the children did not have the proper clothes, they did have the school accessories such as copybooks, pencils, and texts which they had to provide themselves. Sister Priscille told me that parents could not afford to send their children to school and so there was no free education. It was far from being free. And that is what Sister Priscille tried very hard to accomplish. It was to provide resources for some of the children to be able to attend school and become educated and get a job. Sister Priscille is now retired and lives at the convent in Biddeford. She keeps in touch with the nuns in Brazil practicing her Portuguese and encouraging them to persevere in their vocation and mission as helpers within the local communities. She also collects funds for special projects such as enough money to buy sewing machines for the women who are sewing for the poor and neglected orphan children in the Bom Pastor district. She has not returned to Brazil because she tells me that terror attacks are predominant in the Bom Pastor district and the convent has been moved to another area to protect the young nuns and the students. It's truly a sad case of violence and fear of being attacked.

On my second trip to Brazil when we finally received the Fulbright Hays Grant, ten of us, professors and high school teachers departed in June 1993. Each one of us had written a proposal as to why we wanted to go to Brazil and what would be our project. Mine was dealing with *imagens* the sacred folklore figures of the area where we were headed. I wanted to study under the tutelage of a man I had met on my first trip. His name was Antonio Marquez de Carvallo, Professor of the History of Brazilian Art. He was a collector of these figures called *imagens*. He had in his home some forty of these folklore art objects that he had gleaned from different parts of the western part of his province.There were individual figures as well as *oratorios* these shrines for prayers. Antonio spoke French and so I was able to have long conversations with him. He had studied at a seminary in Belgium and that's where he had perfected his French. He told me that most people in his province were poor and could not attend services in church because they lived far from the churches. Therefore, most of them either carved or had someone else carve sacred figurines so that they would be able to have a repository or small chapel in their home. It would be a place of veneration for them. It would replace the church as a place of worship. With time people were able to travel by car, so the little chapels no longer served their purpose. The figurines became art objects and some people sold them for money and made money out of it. Antonio told me that he knew many of these farmers who lived out in the *sertaõ* and he was able to persuade them to sell the art objects to him at a very low price. He told them that their *imagens* were part of their cultural history and they would be sharing their own history with the people. Since many of the owners were friends with Antonio. He knew their parents and grandparents who had created the figurines for the family. He was able to convince them to part with them for cultural purposes. Antonio was a good talker and good listener. Today he has a small museum in Natal where people can go and visit the collection. Many of the figurines are well carved and painted with bright colors. They are truly gems, pieces of folklore art worth a lot of money, I'm sure. What I was able to do was to take photos for slides of the entire collection. At least I would be able to show students as well as people interested in folk art Antonio's collection of Brazilian *imagens*. That was part of my project.

Part of the grant was to visit several areas in Brazil including Natal, We were gone all of July and part of August. From Miami we flew to Rio de Janeiro, then Salvador, Aracaju, Maceio then Recife and finally on to Natal. It was an extremely long flight with several stopovers. We did not know why we had not flown directly to Natal since later on we would return to Salvador and then on to Rio. I was terribly exhausted from the long hours spent flying here and there. We stayed at a small hotel on the Atlantic coast. Sister Priscille came to visit me and I went back to Bom Pastor with her to visit some of the students I had met before. I spent many hours reading books and articles on Brazilian folk art. I discovered that French resembled a lot like Portuguese and so I took many quotes directly in Portuguese. I visited the local university and met several professors such as Professor Ivanilda an anthropologist who was teaching and working at the local folk art museum. She had done her thesis on her hometown patron saint, San Antonio. Although she did not speak a word of English, we managed very well together. I realized then that my Portuguese was improving.

Later on I went back to Jardim de Piranhas with Sister Priscille and another nun, an eight-hour trip by car. We were there three days. Once there, I was introduced to the members of that small community. They worked with the poor and disadvantaged people and I was able to see how terribly poor those people were. They lived in houses with dirt floors and managed to eke out an existence from day to day. The government did not help much except to pass out bags of beans when voting times came around. A local nun asked me what my project was and kept asking me questions about it. Sister Priscille told me later that the other nun wanted to find out about my authenticity and the authenticity of the project, since she was taking me to see one of her close friends and did not want to betray her with a buyer and seller of antique items. Satisfied of my genuineness, she brought us to the home of a lady, a widow who lived alone. She lived in a two-room house with dirt floors. She had on a t-shirt and when she saw me she went into her bedroom to change into her best dress, a poor faded cotton one because she had wanted to be polite in front of an American visitor. We talked with Sister translating for me. The little lady was polite, humble and reverent. We talked about the sacred figurines with which she was familiar. She told me that her dead husband had one and it had been given to him by a relative. We stepped outdoor to say our farewell and the little lady told Sister Priscille that she wanted to give me a wood sculpture. I was stunned. All I could say at that moment was "What?" The lady went back into the house and came out with a small wood sculpture of St. Francis. It was carved a bit primitive-looking and painted brown. I did not know how to reward her. I did not have much money on me. I took off a gold chain with medal around my neck and gave it to her. I knew she would not be able to purchase such an item. She was ever so grateful. She had given me a treasure that had been in the family for so long. A genuine gift from a poor soul whose heart was so generous and giving. I felt humbled and was indeed amazed at her generosity and will ever cherish her gift.

I did spend quite a bit of time with Antonio discussing my project. He advised me to look at it from two vantage points, ICONOGRAPHY and HISTORY. He added that I should also consider legends, religious values, and symbolism. He also suggested that I take into consideration authenticity and tradition. All of this was fodder for my project

One text that I read avidly was Eduardo Etzel's "Imagem Sacra Brasilera" published by Universidade de São Paulo in 1979. He talks a lot about the Virgin Mary under many names such as *Nossa Senhora de Conceicão* and *Nossa Senhora de Soccorro*.[Conception and Sorrow]. Mary is a much revered saint in Brazil and she is honored with so many names. I read many other books dealing with popular art/*arte popular*. I also read that the first Christmas *crèche* was put up in Lisbon, Portugal. In

Brazil, the first nativity scene was set up in 1583 in the sisters' convent in Bahia. That showed the Franciscan influence in both countries.

A very interesting visit was at the local cemetery, *Bom Pastor Cemetario*, not far from the sisters' residence. I went there with a young man I befriended, Francisco. His father was a renowned sculptor. His gravesite looked abandoned. For me it was not a proper grave for such an artistic figure. It seemed to me that that the local area as well as the entire province did not respect their artist sculptors. As I was going out of the cemetery, I looked down and saw a kind of a rag doll lying on the ground. I picked it up and realized that it had pins and needles sticking out. Right away I thought of the voodoo doll. I brought it back to the convent and asked Sister Priscille if it was permitted to handle and even keep such a doll. She told me that quite often people brought such dolls to the cemetery and burned them. Once the ceremony was done, they would leave the voodoo doll there. I could keep it as a souvenir, she said since it no longer belonged to anyone. I first had a trepidation about a voodoo doll in my possession but I brought it with me in my bedroom. When I told the others about this doll, they all insisted that bringing such a voodoo doll on the plane meant bad luck. It was enough to make the plane crash. I laughed and told them that such a thought was superstition and that I intended to bring it home as a folklore artifact. After having a couple of bad dreams, I then decided to get rid of the doll. I brought it back to the cemetery free of any fear of tempting my fate. I did not believe in voodooism, but I was somewhat fearful of the bad vibes it could cause. I was always a timid soul and fearful of nefarious situations.

From Natal, we flew to Salvador on August 6th. Salvador is the capital of the Brazilian state of Bahia. It enjoys a large influence of African culture and its cuisine as well as its music and dance. The first night we were there we went to a restaurant and bar where I had a couple of drinks and ate some meat tidbits although we were warned about eating meat. Meat was considered a carrier of bad effects, we were told. I thought that eating a few pieces would not harm me. But I was wrong. I woke up in the middle of the night with a stomach problem. I felt terribly nauseous. I couldn't even smell food. It made me want to throw up. I tried drinking hot water and even dome coke, but that didn't do anything to my poor stomach. One of my companions went out to the beach area to inquire about my illness with a possible remedy and he came back telling me that coconut milk was the best thing. As soon as I was able to get some, I drank it and it truly alleviated my stomach illness. I slept most of the afternoon and when I woke up I went to a reputable restaurant and had a good meal, *Acarajé:* fried ball of dough made from black-eyed flour with some fruit and shrimps. It is fried in palm oil with a large onion to prevent burning. My stomach was fine. The following morning we all went to the city center where we saw some old homes with balconies and elegant façades. There were many, many vendors out in the streets with kids and adults running to our mini-bus attempting to sell us something in a very aggressive way. I know that it was part of their livelihood but I was not impressed. I simply hated to be hounded by them like flies buzzing all over.

What I learned about Salvador is that there are layers upon layers of cultural values ranging from Portuguese, African[Benin and Nigeria], and Europeans. A true syncretic amalgam of values. That's the way I saw it.

RIO---On the 28th day of our trip to Brazil, August 11, we left very early in the morning and arrived in Rio around nine in the morning. We stayed at the Hotel Acapulco on the Copacabana/Ipanema beaches. My roommate and I went out looking for food. We found several coffee shops and small stores such as the one selling Italian food. We bought lasagna, croissants and a sweetbread with cinnamon and brought it to our room. I went to the beach in the afternoon where I bought a large tangerine from a woman-vendor. Tangerines sold for about 70 cents per dozen. It was the sweetest orange I had ever eaten.

Nighttime was falling on Rio, a dangerous time in our area since it was a red-light district, we were told. My roommate and I did not go too far that evening. The following day we went to Cordevaco, the hill where the huge statue of Christ with the wide open arms stand for all to see. There was a cog-railway type to bring people up the hill. Then there are 217 steps to the statue. It's a very impressive site indeed. One that is seen and recognized all over the world. There are Spanish, French, Italian and English influences and the most recognized branch is the *Carioca*. To be a true Carioca, one must be born in Rio de Janeiro.

After lunch we headed to the *Paõ de agaçuca*[sugarloaf] with a cable/gondola ride to the first "rock". Then on to the "Sugarloaf". It was very high up with a gorgeous view all around us. It was indeed a very impressive experience for me what with the Christ statue and the Sugarloaf that were a sight to see. We were then led to the *Fundaceaõ de Arte Nacional* where I discovered a marvelous bookstore. I bought ten books at very reasonable prices, one a small book on *madeira*[wood] and sculptures. Later on we had a sumptuous lunch at an old opera house across the street from the bookstore. The restaurant had an elegant if not sumptuous décor taken from "Aida." That evening several of us walked the Copacabana beach. It was a quiet, serene and memorable experience simply walking and bringing to mind all the marvelous sites, sounds and food that was part of our trip to Brazil. That night, I wrote in my journal, "Tomorrow we leave for <u>home</u>…good to return to one's private space, out of the group, out of restaurants and hotel living. It's good to go away and enjoy/explore an adventurous venture of sorts, but it's also very good to return home, *chez nous*.

It had been a much appreciated trip since it taught me so many things, first about Brazil and its many varied communities. I enjoyed its people and their warm and welcoming *accueil,* in French. I especially enjoyed my being there in South American charm and delight. I always enjoyed new adventures in learning and experiencing with my eyes, my legs while walking, and my heart in feeling the things that impressed me and stayed with me for a very long time. So long that I can now write about it from memory even if I have some notes to guide me. Notes are fine but nothing compares with the memory finding its splendid recalls of things past. I am so grateful of having a memory that remembers things and sites as well as people that filled my memory and sparks ever-luminescent fireflies of memorable things.

CHAPTER SIX

Theatricality, Pageantry and Cooking

I must not forget to mention one important aspect of my life. From the time where I left off at Fortunes Rocks at seventeen and gradually matured with time and so many experiences I grew to realize that my life was filled with so many memories. I must say that theater, cinema and all kinds of live performances inspired me and revitalized my inner need to wallow in theatricality. I loved pageantry, costumes, great scenes in films such as the coronation of a monarch, the ordination of a bishop, the crowning with the beehive crown of a pope, as well as the playing out of many heroes that had caught my imagination. I have a very active imagination and it serves me well when it comes time to wander into imaginary lands and wonders. I'm not a silly dreamer but a serious and creative person with a very active mind. My mind is never filled with crazy things but rather with meaningful and precious ideas that usually culminate in some written article, a term paper, a short story, a collection of tales or an entire novel once I have found the right topic and stimulating characters. As far as I'm concerned, the brain cannot and must not be still and lazy. It must be active and ever seek new horizons of thought and creativity. Even in my sleep do I get stimulating ideas about what is next in my writing and how can I get answers to my searching and inquisitive mind. The answers come to me either when I suddenly wake up in the middle of the night or when I fully wake up in the morning.

Back to pageantry and theatricality, I have to say that I always loved it and never shied away from it even though I very often hid it in my inner soul. I did not want people to laugh at me and my imagination. Not even my mother who was a practical person. Her scheme of things was pragmatism not idealism. I suppose the land of the ideal was mine to dwell in. I did not love men things such as carpentry tools, sports, and manly uniforms. I did not know how to throw the ball like the male arm does, and I did not like baseball even though this was a real American thing to do. Boys were expected to play baseball and they liked it. It lasted all their lives even through maturity. That went with football and soccer. It was an identifiable tag of belonging to male conformity. I didn't. So I belonged to the isolated genus, isolated in my thoughts and actions. I had to find a place where I could thrive as a creative person. That was the realm of theater, opera, cinema and whatever performing arts that came my way. There I found my niche. There I could enjoy and cultivate my imaginative talents. I am sure that people thought that I was either a sissy, a dreamer or even a silly outsider in society. I didn't care. Well, I did care when I felt alone and out of the picture. I wasn't going to change since I was who I was and could not, would not change a thing. I must say that at times I would have liked to change a few things such as my ability to do man-things, but who was going to show me and teach me how. My father was a humble man, a hard worker and a shy and reclusive person. He didn't play sports and did not go out with the guys. He did love listening to the radio and later watching television, movies and games such as Bulls and Bears and the card game, Flinch. Theatricality was not his cup of tea. He loved war movies and played the part verbally of a general giving orders. He believed in vengeance on the enemy. No pardon, no mercy. He must have liked General Patton very much. I never said a thing to him about it. I doubt that my father would have been that cruel an adversary. He was, after all, a solid Christian who followed the merciful Christ. Did my father fully recognize the mercy of Christ, I've always wondered.

As for pageantry, I loved performers wearing long gowns of silk and satin, capes that flowed from their backs and crowns of gleaming gold with necklaces emblazoning their chests. It just looked elegant and dazzling to me, a poor citizen of the middle-class society. Did I ever wish to be part of the hierarchy or a member of the upper class? I never wished to be part of something I was not due to my birth. Kings and princes are already part of a class that does not merit a lift in society. They're already there unless they abdicate like the Duke of Windsor the supposed-to-be king of England. That Wallis woman made him change his mind. He gave up the throne for the love of a divorcée. What a romantic and useless gesture on his part. That's my opinion.

I liked wearing a cassock once I had taken the habit of the Brothers of the Sacred-Heart in Ancienne-Lorette, Quebec. It had a long pleated scapular topped by a very small hood in the back. It flowed all the way down to the hem of the cassock. To think that in the reform of religious habits called for by Pope John XXIII, most religious communities modified their habits and nuns no longer wore veils and whatever else. The Brothers of the Sacred-Heart eliminated their scapular. How bare did they look after that. Today, most of them do not even wear a habit. They look like regular guys, civilians. I thought that the religious pageantry had been lost in their case and in the cases of so many others. You may call me a show-off and even a glory seeker, but those are my views and feelings about playing an intended part in society and that took some pageantry like wearing the appropriate dress or costume. Actors and performers are fortunate in that they have opportunities of wearing costumes, elegant ones at that, and play a part on stage or in the movies. They become of sorts, someone else only to return to themselves once the performance is over and the applause ceases. They come back to reality or is taking off the costume a step back into reality? What is reality? The stage is by no means reality isn't it? It's a different kind of reality but it's nevertheless its own kind of creative reality. Some may disagree but I remain attached to my sense of idealism and creativity without which life would be damn bland and almost lifeless. I would not want to live in such a world. Give me pageantry, give me LIFE.

Before I get to my writing and my creative self, I want to talk about another form of creativity, that of menus, cooking and baking. I don't know why I had the sense of following menus, recipes, and cookbooks in order to exercise my talents as a chef. Where did I learn how to cook and bake? Who taught me? Was it an innate talent that sprouted from my inner desires to become familiar with the art of making splendid creations of cream, icing, confectioner's sugar, beaten eggs, flour, and any other ingredients that go into the making of cakes and other desserts.

That's what I enjoy the most, making *pâtisserie,* some scrumptious and lovely fabrications of delight. Some prefer the plain, but I prefer the fancy if not elaborate confections. So lovely and delicious that one can hardly dare to cut it and eat it. I also love pies.

My grandmother Laura Beaupré was a tremendous cook. She had started cooking and baking at the age of fourteen. All of her recipes were in her head. If you asked her for a particular recipe, she would say, a pinch of this, a half teaspoon of that, a cup and a half of flour, two eggs, etc. She did all of her cooking on her black stove and her baking in her oven. She knew how to control her oven. She would stoke the coal and add wood to her stove and then she was ready to do whatever she had planned. Some of her best recipes were: first of all her bread with a golden crust, her large crêpe that she placed in her oven, her pies, all kinds of fruit pies including mincemeat, her molasses taffy that she made and pulled for New Year's, her delicious *galettes au pain* cooked in heated lard, and, of course, her pork and beef roasts with *patates* jaunes, golden potatoes swimming in the golden broth. She loved cooking and baking for others. She also loved eating out of her home whenever she was invited, but that was not very often. She was very excited when her son, my uncle Bob, brought her two lobsters to eat. She loved lobsters. All in all, I must have inherited some of my *mémére's* talents for cooking and baking. I never knew my maternal grandmother so I never learned from her. As for my mother, she was the last of thirteen children so she never had the opportunity to learn from her aged mother. She did learn from her mother-in-law, my grandmother Beaupré, but she taught herself and was a good learner.

I enjoy making all kinds of menus for guests that I may have at table. It gives me a chance to be inventive and search for particular recipes that I thought would be delightfully good. The span of my recipes included a *bouilli,* a boiled dinner with a piece of chuck steak, carrots, turnip, string beans and potatoes; salmon pie with red salmon not the pink; *tourtière*/pork pie with vegetables on the side; *fricassée canadienne* that consists of grilled pork chops, onions and cubed potatoes in a brown sauce that my mother used to make; and a delightful stew made with meatballs, carrots and potatoes with tomato soup. Of course I always served a dessert.

I truly loved baking a cake and decorating it with icing and cherries, nuts and raisins depending what I was concocting in my head at the time. I just loved inventing. I cut out recipes or copied them from some book or borrowed some from a friend. Most of all I loved lobster, a Maine staple. Stuffed lobster, boiled lobster, lobster stew and lobster roll were all my favorite things. Of course I also loved clams when they were fresh and small. Not the huge bellied ones. I really liked making a clam chowder or having steamed clams, but most of all I truly delighted in the fried clams, crispy and golden, not overcooked. One thing that my grandmother made that I never tried were *galettes au pain/* fried dough as people call it. She would take a small mound of bread dough and then flatten it so that she could cut strips of dough ready to fry in hot lard. In no time these *galettes* would turn golden and ready to take out of the pan to eat. We the children would eat them with butter or jam. They were soooo delicious early in the morning before school. Of course, when we moved to Hills Beach, we did not have the benefit of grandma's delicacies such as fried dough. She also made her own doughnuts from scratch. They were so good to the taste and so very appealing to the eye and the tummy. I never made or attempted to make doughnuts.

For me recipes are the roadways to accomplishing some delightful creation. There are so many of them. Some handed down from generation to generation. Those are little treasures. They're gems polished by years of trial and error for some. From grandmothers to mothers and from mothers to daughters and, of course, sons. Great chefs are made that way, I believe. Then you have the chef training a son or even a daughter as a chef, but it usually takes years to become an accomplished chef. You have to have it in you. It may be called talent or inner longing to a point where it comes out of your inner self as a real way of expressing yourself. I have learned from others but most of all I have learned through experience. I would say that everything is like that. Education means formation, formation of the mind, the heart and even the soul. I look at soul as the creative force in all human beings. The Blacks know that very well. Soul food, soul music, soul dancing, soul poetry. I let my soul express herself/himself/itself. Whatever. I really do not think that it's "itself" because soul is not a thing. It's divine and it's human at the same time. I'm quite sure. Humanly divine or divinely human, you might say. Outside human sphere there is accommodating inspiration such as nature and everything in it including flowers. That's the quintessential thing in nature as far as I'm concerned. In all his splendor Solomon could not spin the glorious fabric or splendor of a flower. I read that in the gospels. Jesus knew better than to proclaim a man, a king, a very wise king at that than to say that any man, glorious or not can make a flower. Sure he can put seeds in the ground, transplant some or whatever, but he cannot create a flower. Only the Creator can do that. And He sure did it and keeps on doing it right. Grace and talent are given freely to all. It's what we do with them that's so very important in our lives. I sure try very hard to maximize both by cultivating my inner strengths and my God-given talents. Talents can wither away like unwatered, neglected flowers. That's why we have rain and good soil. If neither one is there, then it's disaster. The flowers wither away and die. So many people let their talents curl up withered and die. Talents need life in order to nurture and sing. That's what I think and strongly believe. Enough of that. Let's move on.

Now, I want to talk about clothing in my life. I'm not a peacock nor a cock-a-doodle rooster. I'm not the haughty kind but I do have what we call in French *fierté*, it's self-pride and not a show-off pride. It's very hard to translate well this French term. I know that religious habits prevent those who wear them from choosing different kinds of clothes for each day. They have to wear the habit of their community which is rather simple and plain for most of them. I must admit that some women communities had a more complex habit what with wimples and headgears. Some had extraordinary and complicated head wear instead of a plain black veil. I suppose that some communities wanted something that differentiated them from others. Some sure did such as that community that had a head piece that resembled a huge white fan. Thanks to Pope John XXIII *aggiornamento* meant divesting oneself of all that paraphernalia. He claimed that simplicity and plainness were the order of the day. Get modern and take off tons of long and heavy garments, he said. They sure did up to a point later on they stopped wearing the habits. Plain lay people except for their vows, religious customs and prayers. I missed that customized identity, but I'm sure some people think I'm old-fashioned.

There is a saying in French, *l'habit ne fait pas le moine*, the habit does not make the monk, but it certainly helps to identify who they are and to those outside the community to give the impression that the monk is a venerable monk. But, who knows.

Now back to clothing. I always liked fine clothes, even expensive clothes not from five-and-dime stores like Newberry's or Fishman. I was very selective about fabric, colors, and style. I saved my allowance to be able to pay for what I wanted until I discovered layaway and put-on-my-tab and pay 50 cents a week. I had to be careful about overcharging my account. There was one store Polakewich where they trusted me and expected me to come in every week and pay my 50 cents until I started giving them a dollar. Clothes were cheaper then. Not that the clothes were cheap in quality but cheaper in price. Of course, wages were quite low, for me anyway.

I loved wearing shirt and tie when I went to Sunday mass or any formal getting together like a nuptial dance or an anniversary party. I even wore shirt, tie and sports coat to go to a movie on Sunday evening. Jeans were not in fashion then. Jeans and overalls were for work especially if you worked in the mills. Of course I had one good suit on hand in case I needed it for something special like a wedding. For me, there was something special about getting dressed like a man in a magazine. It showed that a man was worthy of respect and a sense of being more than a laborer. I aspired to become an office worker some day and that took good clothes. I did not think early on of becoming a teacher. That was part of my vocation as a Brother of the Sacred-Heart, but I had given that up when I was sixteen at the novitiate in Canada. I cannot say that I was heartbroken about this, but I had some adjustments that I had to do once out in the "world." Part of that was clothes.

I did not go out much since I had very few friends. I did go to a few dances Saturday nights but did not end up with a girlfriend. The girl I took to a dance was but a partner. You could not go to a dance without a girl. Some tried to go alone with the possibility of finding one at the dance, but that never worked for me. I was too shy and timid of being refused if I dared to ask someone to dance with me. It was a real challenge for me. Not having been to school dances, I did not know how to mingle and talk to girls. I mean the routine of dating and going out with girls. But, I knew I was well-dressed and I did impress the girls. Someone had told me so. The clothing made the man and I was aware of that.

Thanks to my mother, my clothes were always washed and ironed. She was also a proud person, my mother, and she made sure that all creases in shirts were flattened out and the pants well pressed. Washed clothes and dried outdoors on the clothesline smelled so good and fresh. Just like linen on the line. It smells so good when you go to bed and you can smell the freshness of the sheets and pillow cases. Of course, I realize that clothing does not necessarily make the man, but it sure helps to uphold his sense of pride and well-being, être *fier dans sa peau/* to be proud in one's skin, is the French saying for being proud of oneself and rightly so.

For me, theatricality, pageantry, *fierté* and clothing as well as good appearance and inner glow from a satisfaction well-deserved goes together like a hand in glove. The hand feels right and the glove fits well. They all complement one another as in a symphony or a well-arranged presentation of whatever kind. Quality and precision is of utmost importance since you have to give great care to what is being done and orchestrated. It must sound true and perfect in harmony. You see, I'm a perfectionist, an idealist. You must know that by now. A sense of idealism is a sense of aiming high. Never look down, never wallow in the mud. However, as Baudelaire says, *Tu m'as donné ta boue et j'en ai fait de l'or/* speaking of Paris, You gave me your mud and I turned it into gold. Mud into gold, that's what poetry does.

CHAPTER SEVEN

A Good Friend. The Artist

At this juncture, I have to talk about a very good friend of mine, probably the very best I ever had. Her name was Micheline B. Friends like her are rare. Friends like that are the glue that bonds people together indeed. It's the best of all adhesives. Friends like that never come unglued, never separate themselves from *l'amitié particulière/ special friendship*. I knew right away that we would eventually bond like two agents that cannot ever be separated. Agents of love and caring, not a physical love but a love beyond Platonism and closer to mystical and sacred attachment. It was meant to be, I suppose, but I sincerely believe that it was not only meant to be but long awaited in my heart of hearts, almost soul-like. When someone says soul-friend, I firmly believe in that to a point where I can honestly say I have discovered one in my lifetime. I'm sorry to have to say that I lost her to some kind of tragedy, but I will explain later on once you get to know her.

She was born in the U.S., in New England a daughter of Franco-American heritage. She spoke fluent French and was a perspicacious, intelligent, and sagacious child. She grew up in the Jansenistic tradition with a father and mother who maintained a rigid sense of adherence to the rules of religion and of society. She said that she was a rebellious child, a creative child full of the power of the imagination who cannot adhere to rules. Her mother's cautious words to her was, *Fais pas ton énervée* / Don't misbehave or be wild, don't act up, don't be mischievous. It's hard to translate. Not that she was all of that, but she could not stand her mother's nagging her all the time. She told me once that since her father was a doctor, both her father and mother expected her to behave like a doctor's child, polite, well-behaved, respectful of adults, always obligingly obedient, ever smiling and demure as a girl should be and ever, yes ever proper. Micheline could not swallow all of that. It was not her, she told me, it was not part of her fabric as a woman. So she rebelled hoping to cast aside an identity that was not hers. What to do? Well her parents sent her far away to a convent near Montreal. That's what parents with a rebellious child used to do in the past. *Fais pas ton énervée* meant if you do not behave like we want you to behave, a proper child of two professionals[her mother played the violin in an orchestra] then we must see to it that someone will reform you or even mold you the way it should be. And that was the role of nuns in their estimation. They were trained as such, obedient, rigid in their adherence to rules and never *énervées*. Never irritatingly on someone's nerves. Never ever. They were nuns. Nuns are taught to be complacent, rigidly obedient and unnerved by whatever commotion they experience. They're nuns, for God's sake.

Micheline stayed with the nuns at the convent three and a half years until her father came to get her and bring her yet to another convent in upper state New York. After three and a half years at the former convent, the nuns there found her to be not malleable at all. They said that she was as stubborn as a mule and they could not control her. They could not make her understand that she had to follow the rules of the convent and not disobey Mother Superior. That she was a strong-willed student and could not bend to follow whatever discipline imposed on her. She was considered an undisciplined teen. A girl unable to meet the demands of rules and discipline. *Une énervée, c'était tout!* So she was sent away in spite of her pleading and strong promises of her aims to please whomever. She wound up in a village unknown to most people, a village in upper New York where the population was 58 people, 47 farmers and wives, no children and 3 cows. The only convent around took care of twelve girls as boarding students. It was truly a remote village with the train stopping there once a week to deliver a few passengers and pick up a few more. Micheline did not like that place at all. She told me that she was considered a rebel and an overzealous fighter for students' rights. The nuns granted no rights just courteous obligations to seek what students wanted for study and nourishment. Even then, the nuns controlled almost every single thing. It was their right to do so, they claimed. Micheline hated that convent. Even though she complained to her parents, she realized that her letters were "sanitized" before being sent. No results happened. She told me that it was an impossible situation. She stopped writing. Her father came up to see what was happening and she told him that she could not explain. The father then decided to send her to another school. This time it was not a convent. She finished high school as a salutatorian.

Micheline had applied to several colleges and she chose one in upstate New York. She wanted to major in Social Studies. She made a lot of friends and even had a boyfriend. She was all excited about her new life and she got pregnant, another link in her rebelliousness against her parents. She decided not to have an abortion. She gave the child up to an adoption agency. The child was a girl. She never saw her. After graduation she got a job in an agency dealing with orphans. She met this young man who wooed her into marriage never informing her parents about it. He was Jewish and she had been raised as a Catholic. It was as it was known then a mixed marriage. Her parents would have disapproved of it. She had two daughters, Mia and Monique and tried to raise them without the help of her husband whom she called "a lamebrain." There was no love between them. She got several small jobs but none that pleased her. She was getting desperate when she got the idea of getting away from all things including her country. She was going to a place where it would be warmer than northern United States. She chose France because French was her native language even though her children did not speak a word of French. They would learn easily, she told me. She arrived in Nice and decided to go to Monaco to get a job with the Jacques Cousteau Institute of Oceanography. She got a small house on the seashore in Nice thanks to two unmarried sisters who felt sympathy for her and her two young daughters. Besides, she spoke French. They thought she was French-Canadian. She sent her daughters to a local school all the time teaching them French. It's was easier being surrounded with all French-speaking people and being immersed in the French culture. Micheline felt truly at home in Nice.

She occasionally wrote to her mother and even thought of bringing her children someday to visit her parents.

That's how I first met her. I was in the process of putting together a Winter Term course for January 1985 and needed more participants since I only had three students signed up for a course in French Impressionism. I had decided to go to France and include a visit to southern France to study Renoir at his place of work as a painter, Cagnes-sur-Mer. So, I advertised in the local papers for students interested in joining me in my cultural expedition. I did not expect too many responses since the cost would not necessarily attract too many people. That's what I told myself. I did get a telephone call from a Mrs. B, Micheline's mother who informed me that her daughter lived there and she would be glad to give me her phone number and address in Nice. Nevertheless I did get a participant, an adult student who wanted to come along. So I had three college students, one adult participant and one contact in Nice. That was enough to allow the course to go on.

We arrived in Paris and visited the Impressionist museums, the Galerie nationale du Jeu de Paume and l'Orangerie as well as other sites in and around Paris. We then took the train to Nice. Once we were established in our hotel, I planned to go to Cagnes-sur-Mer to visit Renoir's museum. Unfortunately, it was closed. We had come so far and gotten no results. I did not despair. I reached Micheline and got a welcoming response saying that her mother had already told her about me. We planned to meet at a restaurant in Nice. I made reservations for an evening reception with cake and wine. When I first saw Micheline, she seemed a bit shy and somewhat inquisitive as to why I was in Nice. I explained it to her and we started a long conversation. I could see that the students were not too interested in her, and so I told them they could leave and do whatever they wanted. My conversation with Micheline lasted into the night. I was impressed by her story and her adventures into finding herself and her art. She told me that she was not an artist by training and that she had a different perspective on art than most artists that she knew. She was into watercolors. Why? Because she liked the way watercolors flow down the special paper she purchased for her watercolors. It dripped by itself and showed her the way, the direction it was going and thus wanted her to go as an artist. She loved colors.

She adored colors. We became friends and as the years flowed I got to meet her over and over at her small house in Varengeville-sur-mer where Monet had painted his "Hut in Trouville, low tide" and "The Pines in Varengeville," as well as other paintings. Monet loved the outdoors and painted with delight and freedom from enclosures in Varengeville.

From Nice where she was shoved out of her place by one of the sisters, she moved in with two friends in Nice until such time she was able to afford to go and live near Paris. It was a kind of government housing with many people living close together. She could not stand being in a beehive of living quarters. She was outside her element, she told me. What was her element, I asked her. "I want to live with the freedom of a gitane/gypsy, and free to paint and do whatever I wish." She did paint and she did find a place in Varengeville where she felt comfortable in the location so often adopted by artists such as Monet. She would try to earn money by selling her watercolors. She would try very hard at it over and over again but with not very much success. She needed a publicist, she also needed a marketing agent, she insisted. I tried repeatedly to encourage her and sent her occasionally some money to help her pay for artist's supplies. She was ever grateful since she was poor without an income. Some people told her to get a job but she refused to spend her time looking and not finding. She told them that she was an artist and did not want a job. She had one. I totally agreed with her. She once told me that quite often she had just enough bread to feed the two daughters and quite often she went to bed hungry. It broke my heart.

I interviewed her in Nice and recorded the conversation. She talked about her dream of being an accepted artist and why she painted watercolors and not oils at the moment. She set up workshops on art and creativity and traveled long distances where she met with small groups of women who wanted to learn from her. She was adamant about having these women step out of the box, as she called it, and dare to create artistically even if it meant not doing it traditionally and habitually. She would pack her things and take the train to wherever she was going like the southeastern part of France. Most of the time she spent several days away from home. She received a small remuneration but not enough to support herself and purchase her art supplies. She did not mind since she made new friends and delved into new ventures in painting and teaching.

Here is what she told me about her philosophy of art with watercolors. "Art is not only putting colors on paper, canvas or any other substance. When I paint with watercolors, I do it because it's not easy; it's hard work. Many artists stay away from it. I'm hardheaded and so I do it to prove to myself and others that I can do it and succeed in the process. Art must start in the guts, go up through the veins and arteries then come out through the fingers and flow with a sense of *fierté* and vigor." That was essentially her creative expression on art as she saw it and experienced it. She was a gutsy lady, I told her, and she laughed.

Her basic ideas on art were cast into stone so-to-speak. That is, they were hard and solid, irreplaceable. They had been born of a fiery vigor spun in the heart and soul of a firm believer in the freedom of both art and the artist. She felt that without freedom, without a free and open mind, there cannot be true art. The artist does not need a dogma nor a set of rules. Everything must flow freely and without obstructions such as societal regulations. True art, she stated, must be true to itself in its expression. The artist is but the vehicle, the modem operandi. Strongly influenced by color field and lyrical abstract artists of the 50's and 60's, her work has always been non-figurative. She says, and I quote, "My non-figurative style remains resolutely free, without dogma, without system, without formal solutions. The subject remains the 'experience' of painting itself." And, she adds, "My research lies in the constant exploration of the expressive power of colour, the cornerstone of my work. The orchestration of colour contrasts gives rise to forms, lines and movements during the creation process."

Micheline's last series of paintings was called **Bleu de BLEUES**. She had put in a lot of work, physical labor just setting it up at the Médiathèque de Garenne Colombes, region Parisienne. That was in the fall of 2016. I had a conversation with her in Paris over the phone in the hotel where I was staying. That was the last conversation we had except for a few e-mails later on. She told me that she was extremely proud of this series since it represented all of her creativity as an artist. However, she was dead tired with a bad back. She was returning to her home in Varengeville to get some much-needed rest. Unfortunately, the sales were meager. She began to think that all had been in vain. What was the use of painting without much encouragement, without money to pay for the art supplies, and especially to buy food. Discouragement, despair set in. Would she ever find some measure of success, both artistic and financial was the crucial question. It was not a matter of failing in the expression of her art but rather in her failure of getting a good publicist/marketing agent to sell her work. She had tried repeatedly but her efforts were in vain since she had no valid contacts. This led her to constant struggles and dire situations in her quest for living without setbacks. In her last e-mails to me she indicated that she was contemplating assisted suicide. She knew this woman who through word of mouth was known to assist people who chose the path of death as a release. She had forewarned her daughters about her intention to someday get out of her misery by a quick and painless death. She talked about the possibility of making an end to everything in her listless living in several e-mails to me. I tried very hard to insist that she had a lot to live for. She argued that when the time comes, she would know. I could hear the cry of despair in her words to me and I sensed her decision to put an end to it all even her art that had motivated her all her life. Then everything stopped. No more e-mails no more conversations not even a word from the daughters. I tried, I really tried, but nothing. I take it as a farewell. *Adieu, chère amie de coeur et d'âme.*

CHAPTER EIGHT

My writing

I have come to the final chapter of putting in writing my story as a writer from the beginning to my retirement from university teaching. I decided to quit teaching and retire early because I had had it with trying to teach students literature. In my last literature course, "The Solitary Hero" based on three novels, **Les Misérables**, **Germinal** and **The Grapes of Wrath**. I wanted to compare and contrast all three authors, Hugo, Zola and Steinbeck and their well-known works. *Les Misérables* is a work of romantic influence and depicts a Jean Valjean struggling with a society oftentimes giving him the pains and misery of living in a cruel world. With *Germinal* and "Grapes of Wrath" I wanted to show students the similarities of naturalism in literature. I spent a lot of time in the preparation for this course. I was determined to give it my all and attempt to make the students love literature by reading and discussing great novels. The day came and it was the first day of class. I soon realized that some had not even purchased the books. One student told me that he was going to borrow another student's books and that he was not going to buy them. I was more than surprised. After all, all they had to buy was three books. After two or three weeks, I realized that several students did not do the prescribed readings. Most of them were either physical or occupational therapy majors and I knew that this course was not one that satisfied their hunger for learning. It was an elective and they were trying to satisfy their humanities requirement. I was totally dismayed and disappointed with the entire class except for one English major who did all of the readings and participated in the discussions. Her name was Maureen M. Oftentimes she was the only one participating even though I tried to get the other students involved. It was like encountering a blank wall or rather a stone wall of indifference. I later learned that what the students were interested in was the final grade and their GPA. One student even asked me what did it take to get an "A" in the course. I told him that I did not simply give out grades. Students had to earn them. That's what made me retire early. I did not want to have this experience again. I loved teaching and I loved literature, but I did not to want teach any courses where students were not going to be actively participating in the readings and discussions. It was a stalemate position for me as a teacher. I could no longer take it. I told the Dean and the department that I was going to retire after the semester. It was the Fall semester of 1999.

That's when I devoted myself and most of my time to my writing. I had already started to write earlier while teaching a full load. I must state here that my very first writing began in 1956. I sent a contribution to the Reader's Digest "First Person Story" and it was not accepted. It was my first and last submission. I did not write for several years although the rejection did not totally discourage me. I thought that I would have to mature in my writing abilities before I could write for another magazine or a publisher. I must say that I did not even consider a publisher. I did not think then that I was qualified to do so. It would take years to submit anything to a publisher. Then I would realize how difficult it would be to find a publisher. One that would even consider anything that I wrote.

Before I go on, I have to talk about publishing and publishers. Publishing is the most difficult thing to do for a writer like me. First, you are told that you must have an agent. Well, I tried to find one. I looked in several volumes at our local library and chose a few names and addresses. I then mailed my request. I received no acceptance. Each one told me that they had enough clients and could not take anymore. There goes my chance to get published, I told myself. I never attempted to find an agent again. Eventually I did find what was then called a "vanity press." Now it is called "self-publication" with a fee attached to it. Thanks to a friend of mine, I found one in Florida, Llumina Press. My friend encouraged me to submit my first manuscript to them. I did.

It was **Marginal Enemies**. It was accepted for publication in 2002. This book was conceived in Berlin, Germany while I was spending some time with the father of a former student of mine. From Berlin, I planned to go to Paris for my sabbatical research. I had just visited the former Olympic stadium in Berlin where I had not seen any remnant of Nazi identification on its walls. I thought it was a bit strange but then I realized that Germany wanted to erase that ignominious part of the past as much as it could. While in my bedroom, I started thinking about the concept of enemy. Are women and children considered enemies in a war, I thought. That's the very beginning of my book.

I must say that there was a publication prior to this one. It's a book about a wood carver named Adelard Coté from Biddeford. He was a folk carver who carved animals. This book has a bilingual text, French and English, with several photos taken by my then neighbor, Stephen Muskie, who had an M.F.A. degree from the Rochester Institute of Technology. It was published under the auspices of the National Materials Development Center in Bedford, N.H. in 1982. I was proud of my first publication, a folk art book. It has become a collector's item.

My first novel was written in French since I wanted to prove to myself and others that I could do it. Besides, French was my maternal language. It's a book about my growing up. It's one of my favorites, *Le Petit Mangeur de Fleurs,* [The Little Flower Eater]. The original title was "The Little Eater of Bleeding Hearts" but the publisher did not like it since he thought of blood and daggers. He did not recognize the fact that bleeding hearts are flowers. The eating of these flowers here is the metaphor for the child eating his esthetics based on the story my mother told me about my childhood days. I eventually translated it and it was published.

My second work is a collection of tales with pen and ink drawings. The title is *Lumineau,* a word that I invented since I wanted a word that merged light and water. The book contains nine tales that I drew out of my imagination. The first one deals with the legend of the milkweed. When I was young I had a very active imagination. You see, I thought that hiding in the green pod of the milkweed was a little bird, but when I opened one up, I realized that there was nothing but a handful of silken threadlike things. It was published by JCL in Chicoutimi,

Québec in 2002. The same publisher that published "The Little Eater" in 1999. That was the end of my writer/publisher relationship with JCL since the publisher did not want to publish my books anymore. The first two had not sold well.

My next book was another publication in French, **Deux Femmes, Deux Rêves,** a novel based on my mother's and maternal grandmother's story. When I started thinking about writing, I thought of writing an epic about the entire story of the French-Canadians emigrating to New England. It was a huge project that I was contemplating. It was historical, cultural and sociological in range. I started writing it long hand and showed what I had to a friend. She told me that all I had written about were women. I then realized that I was in the wrong scheme of things. I wasn't writing an epic at all. I was writing a story based on my mother's and maternal grandmother's story as I had lived it with stories that my mother had told me. That's when I changed the title[the original title was **Au Fil de l'Eau**]. The grandmother is nostalgic, romantic while the daughter is realistic and thinks of the future, not the past. It's a novel that's ninety percent biographical. It was published in 2005.

Next came a dramatic monologue in French. I chose to write it in our dialect taking a chance that it would succeed. Antonine Maillet, the well-known Acadian writer had written her play, **La Sagouine** in her own dialect and succeeded very well. It was a popular success with hundreds of performances throughout Canada and even the U.S. She told me that she had taken a chance by writing in her dialect. So, I say that I did the same thing. I also took a chance that people would accept it. I had been raised and educated knowing full well that our dialect was only good for speaking at home and in the neighborhood. I was especially sensitive to the situation since I now had a Ph.D. from a prestigious university and I was expected to only use and speak the standard accepted French. What will people think, I asked myself. Well I did it and it was very well received here in New England as well as Québec. It's about a retired mill worker spilling out her thoughts and feelings about work in the mills and the experiences she had as an uneducated socially marginal person. It was published in 2006. Later on, I translated it for people who did not understand French but wanted to read my play.

I had a very bright student in my Basic French class. He came from Pennsylvania and he wanted to major in medical sciences. He was very opened to the humanities. He excelled in my course and I still maintain to this day that he was the best student with the very best French pronunciation I ever had. He graduated valedictorian of his class and went on to apply at the medical school at Temple University. He was not accepted. He was greatly disappointed and he sought a job in the health care field. He hopped from job to job even accepting a job as manager of a video and recording store. He had many a struggle with his identity as a man in search of himself. He had a few relationships with a woman but they did not pan out. He thought of becoming a home decorator but could not afford the cost of tuition and other fees. He truly loved the fine arts. He thought of joining me in Paris during my stay there. It failed because the French government had just imposed the rule of visas for all visitors since there had been a terrorists attack at a store called, Tati. Besides the airline fees had jumped up to an exorbitant price that he could not afford. Later on, he contracted AIDS telling me that he had tried to help a man lying in the street and was pricked by a needle that was being used as he was helping the poor man. He went to several doctors but in the end he died of the disease. I got to know all of that plus more details of his life when we started corresponding. I kept all of his letters to me. I truly loved this young man. I suspected that he was gay and had gotten the deadly virus that way but he never admitted that. I did not want to shame him nor have him feel guilty of a dangerous relationship. He admitted to me in one of his letters that he had contemplated suicide. He never went to the ultimate end of it. He said that he had had a mystical experience of sorts and it changed his way of thinking about living and dying. The title of the book is **Before All Dignity Is Lost** and the phrase is taken from one of his letters. In the book, I call him "the bad luck kid." The book was published in 2006. The sales were poor. However, I did get a letter from a young lady who said she was in tears after reading my book. That was rewarding for me. I had touched someone with my writing.

One of the Deans of my university whose name was Mike M. truly inspired me and gave me insights into the art of teaching and motivational training. He was a highly intelligent person and a man with thirty-three thoughts in his head all at the same time, he said. He was always thinking creatively about the next project he was going to undertake. He had come to New England because he wanted to get as far as he could from Oklahoma where his wife had died in an auto accident. He had one daughter who was a young teenager.

He entertained a keen interest in the Native American culture and he had established a close relationship with several members of this ethnic group including Wilma Mankilller, the first woman to be the principal chief of the Cherokee nation.

Mike loved the southwest territory and had become one of the trustees of the Ghost Ranch in Abiquiu, New Mexico. This territory was Georgia O'Keefe's territory of artistic inspiration. One day he invited me to accompany him on a trip to New Mexico in order to visit some areas and people he knew well but also to get acquainted with the Ghost Ranch. While he was attending a long meeting at the ranch, I was able to visit the desert area associated with the Ghost Ranch. I took my camera with me since I wanted to keep a visual record of my visit. While there I got interested in the bright sunlight, the desert hues, the cacti and flowers, the deadwood and the rock formation. I took many photos and returned home inspired by what I had seen and experienced enough to write a book about it. I entitled the book, **Trails Within, Meditations on the Walking Trails at the Ghost Ranch in Abiquiu, New Mexico**. Published in 2007. I turned my photos into color slides so as to be able to show a slide show to students and faculty. The slides were used for my book as illustrations. In this book I state and I quote, "This is essentially a book of reflections on particular ways of seeing things on the three walking trails at the Ghost Ranch in Abiquiu, New Mexico…walking trails, holistically speaking, are the occasions for physical exercise, emotional release, esthetic activity, intellectual operation, and spiritual excursion." I continue to say that the word soul is employed "to mean the creative power in all of us, potential as well as active." This is a work I truly relish and find my honest and transparent self at work within the core of the humanities.

Next comes a sequel to my dramatic monologue, ***La Souillonne***, since I was asked if there was a follow-up to it since so many readers had enjoyed the play and its speaker/character. The title is ***La Souillonne, deusse***. It's a continuation of the stories the old mill worker weaves together. Published in 2008.

Then came my book on Van Gogh. I had taught a course on French Impressionism after having been to Paris several times and enjoying the offerings of the large museums there. I learned a lot from my visits and followed up on them with much reading especially on the French Impressionists. Later on I also did research and read several books on the American Impressionists since I was giving a course during the Summer months to Elderhostel participants.

I had never really appreciated Van Gogh and his temper and rebelliousness as well as his paintings. I thought they were outside the art world that I knew. They were exceedingly bold in color and so very different from what I knew about paintings, from the Renaissance to the Impressionists. I liked paintings that represented reality and true form. I liked the value of light in an Impressionist painting. I especially liked a follower of the Impressionist movement, Gustave Caillebotte and his painting ***Les Raboteurs de Parquet***. This work is so true to life and so well crafted that it impressed me as a work of art. However, I began to recognize the strong value of bright light in Van Gogh's works. That's why he moved to the southern part of France where the light is so much brighter. I also began to appreciate such works as ***La Nuit Étoilée*** / Starry Night and ***Les*** Tournesols/The Sunflowers. Van Gogh's paintings have to enter your soul and esthetic self before you can enjoy his art and his skill as a painter. That's the way I feel. And so, I decided one day to write a book about Van Gogh in Arles. I gave it the title of **The Boy With the Blue Cap** after a painting he did called **Portrait of Camille Roulin**. The boy is Joseph Roulin's, son. Joseph Roulin was an *entreposeur des postes*, a sort of postman working for the railroad. Van Gogh did a few paintings of him dressed in his bold blue uniform with shiny gold buttons. Van Gogh liked the Roulin family. Joseph Roulin and his wife, Augustine were kind to him.

I decided to use the boy, Camille, as my vehicle in telling the story of Van Gogh in Arles. Everyone knows that Van Gogh was not very much liked in Provence. He had no friends except for the Roulin family. So I thought that taking the boy, Camille, and having him follow the lone wolf painter and showing him what and how he painted would be an exciting and unusual way of delving into the artist at work in the luminosity of the land. I even bring Van Gogh to Saintes-Maries-de-la-mer where the gypsies came to pray each year during their festival of la Camargue in front of the statue of the black saint, Sara-la-kâli. I remember going there myself and meeting a gypsy woman who offered me a medal proffering her hand for an offering. When I tried to give her a two-franc piece, she took the coin but took back her medal. I was surprised at her gesture of

I also bring the father Roulin and his son Camille to visit Van Gogh at the asylum in Saint-Rémy where he painted "Starry Night" and so many other memorable paintings. Finally, Van Gogh leaves Arles and takes the train to Paris and winds up eventually in Auvers-sur Oise.

I had a great experience in doing the research for and then writing this book. I had truly gotten into it and took a tremendous delight in describing each painting I wrote about in detail. For me it was like recreating the painting itself. Each stroke of the brush, each color, and each subject matter was defined with my choice of words. I thought I had succeeded very well through the intermediary of a boy named Camille Roulin who wore a blue cap.

Following the publication of this book, I made a trip to Arles simply to confirm the locations I had used in my book. Then I took another trip, this time to Amsterdam particularly to see the actual painting of the "Portrait of Camille Roulin." It's a small painting and it's right there on the wall of the Van Gogh's Museum in Amsterdam. I stood in front of it amazed and filled with the joy that I had created a novel based on that specific painting. The boy, Camille, would probably be delighted that I made him a gifted person and a fine writer. And of course, a very good friend and student of the famous artist, Vincent Van Gogh.

I realized at one point that Franco-American writers like myself did not have many opportunities to get published. So, I decided to gather some tales and stories written by Franco-American authors that I knew and have them published as an anthology by my publisher. It would give these authors a venue for their writings. I got ten participant authors with eleven stories, all in French. I added four of my compositions with a poem by Normand Dubé, a poet who passed away several years ago. I decided to call the work, ***Voix Francophones de Chez Nous***. It was published in 2009. Without a publicist and a marketing director, the anthology was not a success. I was hoping that certain schools and colleges would find an interest in it in teaching Francophone literature but it did not happen. There are successes and failures in life although I never considered this book a failure.

My next book was a translation of ***La Souillonne, monologue sur scène.*** I did it because some people wanted to read it and could not read French. Then I decided to write a novel based on the life and work of Émile Friant, an Alsatian author who was not very well appreciated in France but a realist painter whose paintings became better known in the U.S. due to a very good and well-respected art dealer, Paul Durand-Ruel. I had seen the movie, <u>*Il y a longtemps que je t'aime,*</u>[I've Loved You For a Long Time]. directed by Philippe Claudel in which there was a painting by Friant called ***La Douleur.*** We see an old woman dressed all in black stooped over an open grave in the local cemetery of Préville. Another woman also in black clothing is standing next to her. The pain and grief on the old woman's face made me empathize with her and put a big lump in my throat. I truly felt for her. The artist had done a superb job at portraying this sad but dignified scene of sorrow. I learned that the artist was Émile Friant. I decided then and there that I would write a novel based on his life and his work. I had done it with Van Gogh and had truly enjoyed doing this writing project. So I was going to repeat my performance as a writer and write about another artist. There was very little written about Friant and I had to search a lot of places to try and find some materials on Friant, the realist painter. I found a few and my internet search gave me several leads to information that I could use. Of course, I could invent stuff since this was going to be a novel. The cultural history of Alsace-Lorraine and Paris furnished me with good background material. I was able to use the cultural and historical facts that I gathered such as the Universal Exposition of 1889 followed by the World's Fair in 1890 as well as the Salons of Paris where artists were invited to show their works. The more I found out about Friant the more I was intrigued with his art and his life experiences. Where there were gaps in his life story, I added some characters and some actions that revitalized his story such as the meeting with Angelo, a close friend from Italy who tries to show him sensuality. Here is a novel that combines both biography and creativity of invention. The novel was published in 2010.

My next literary effort was the translation of *"Le Petit Mangeur."* Translation is a difficult skill but knowing French and English well, I mastered the art of translation in this book. This was followed by an attempt on my part to deal with an entirely different kind of book. I wanted to write some spiritual reflections based on the gospels. My theme was "simplicity." The title became **Simplicity in the Life of the Gospels---Spiritual Reflections**, published in 2011. It was a good exercise in meditation and spirituality. I reread the gospels and took notes on anything that touched upon the concept of simplicity. I knew that Christ was a man/god given to the simple life and preached simplicity by his own life on earth. He expressed a definite aversion to the lack of simplicity and especially to the pharisaic duplicity of those who were haughty and filled with self-pride. Christ's message of love resonates throughout the gospels and leads one to believe that the New Covenant is a message of love couched in simplicity. At least that's what I believed and wrote about. The book is a call to simplicity. I say and I quote, "The thread of simplicity has led me, not out, but deep inside the bowels of the good news." Adding "Simplicity becomes a foil to the entanglements of those who wish to obstruct or deny the good news." The book is from the perspective of a literary person such as myself, and not from the pen of a theologian or an exegete. It's about that time that I discovered the talented artist, Jean Keaton and her great drawings. I was granted permission to use some of them taken from the collection, "As I have loved you." They add to my text a marvelous merging of Christ with people from babies to young adults. The cover reveals a playful Jesus making kids laugh. I found that so very human and filled with truth and simplicity.

Next was my attempt to follow up on my *Soullionne* books and wrote a book entitled, ***Madame Athanase T. Brindamour, histoires et folleries***, published in 2012. It's a book about stories as told by a Franco-American woman and her husband in our local dialect. It wasn't as successful as the *Souillonne* books but I did succeed in refocusing on my native tongue which is colorful and in a way that is expressive of our cultural values.

Then came a major project in my writing, that of depicting the construction of a Gothic cathedral in the Middle Ages. I had attended a summer workshop in Paris l'*Île-de-la-Cité*, under the auspices of a grant administered by Columbia Professor, Stephen Murray, a specialist in Gothic cathedrals. Each participant had a project and mine was the Green Man or the Foliate Head. My favorite was the Green Man of Bamberg, in Germany. He appears in many cathedrals in France, Great Britain and Germany. We visited several cathedral sites in and around Paris. It was in Amiens where Professor Murray showed us what Gothic space was. He had us look way up to the ceiling of the Cathedral, close our eyes to then reopen them while walking up the center aisle and never looking down and breathe in this vast and open space that he called Gothic space. It was a dizzying but marvelous experience that I had never had before. One can surely feel the space created by the Gothic architect. I truly enjoyed this course given by an admired and cognizant professional. He had several contacts and we were able to have the selected cathedral opened up for us by the local caretaker with keys that he had in his care. We walked up to the roofs and climbed the many arches to get a better view of the intricacies of the building while being able to have a good view o the flying buttresses called in French, *les arcs boutants,* a much more accurate name according to Professor Murray. There's nothing "flying" about them, he said.

After the completion of our stay in Paris, I returned home to file my written project to Washington. Then I decided to write a novel about the construction of a Gothic cathedral. I called it ***Cajetan, the Stargazer.*** It's the story of a young architect, Cajetan, who goes through the stages of the guilds and eventually builds a cathedral of his own. I used my knowledge of Gothic cathedrals that I had gained in France during my summer studies with Professor Murray to construct a realistic story of an architect building a cathedral and all the various stages he has to go through. I used my creative imagination based on facts and figures dealing with architecture and stone cutting with the art of sculptures including the art of the glaziers making colorful windows for the church. I was amazed at the long and dedicated hard work that all the workers went through including the wise and knowledgeable strength of the architect directing the construction that took several years to complete. This work is one of my very best as a novel. It was published in 2013.

L'Étranger extraterrestre is my novel about extraterrestrial happenings and a young man who meets a so-called alien from another planet. It's not a sci-fi novel as such but a novel that touches upon dimensions of philosophy, cosmology, astronomy, theology and myth. Pascal, the main character, meets Andraiü Kaltfeuer from the fourth cycle at the sixth domain in the universe. His existence, he says, is linked to the fates of the stars for his birth was mysterious. It was tied to galaxies, stars and nebulous presences. Pascal gets his calling from the extraterrestrial one who commands him to go on a quest for the Absolute and declares him a prophet. He first meets the Wise One, a seer, then to a monastery, followed by an encounter with an artist named Cassandra, then to a woman, Marjolaine-the Healer, and finally to a man called Theophilus afflicted with dementia who has extraordinary moments of lucidity. This novel is my venture into the extraterrestrial not always knowing where I was going and what I was seeking. Who knows the power of the creative mind? What attempts can be made to uncover the mystery of Creation and the Absolute? Do scientists know how, humanists and philosophers? Any other being on earth? Perhaps we have to go beyond our world to strive at arriving at answers to the BIG questions. This work was published in 2013.

Marie-Quat'e-Poches et Sarah Foshay, Dialogue à *Deux Faces* is my attempt at reconciling the dialect and the standard French. It's a sort of tour-de-force in motion. Two young women have long conversations dealing with cultural heritage, language and personal identity. The mysterious part of the story is that one of the characters is a revenant. It's a novel that explores the richness, the value, the importance of the heritage of a collectivity known as Franco-American. One could say that this is the author's manifesto on cultural identity. Published in 2013.

In Search of the Fallen Divina---Maria Callas, is a novel dealing with a young man from northern Maine who is conducting a search for the diva, Maria Callas who lives in isolation in Paris. I knew very little about la Callas until my friend Roger G. introduced me to her operas and her life story. At first, I did not like the diva and her signing although she was highly recognized as a supreme star of opera throughout the world. It was by reading the librettos while listening to the music that I got to appreciate her voice and the dramatic if not tragic quality of her renditions. Later on while watching Tom Hanks commenting on the aria, ***La Mamma Morta*** in the engrossing film, "Philadelphia" that I realized the striking quality of Callas's singing. I could feel the deep warmth and sharp tension of a mother's death in the heart of a daughter who was protected by the mother during the turmoil of the French Revolution. That rendition struck me so much that I knew I had to write something about Maria Callas. But what? So much had been written about the Divine Diva. I decided to take a different angle to the telling of the story I wanted to write. I did a lot of reading and research and came up with ideas, facts and fiction on Maria Callas. I certainly did not want to get caught up in the Aristotle Onassis episodes in Callas's life.

For me three words denote the thrust of a written work: inspiration, subject matter and treatment. After a while after having written as many books as I have, it's not easy getting the inspiration that gives one the subject matter for a book. I realize that there are many possibilities, but which one is *abordable* as we say in French. Which one is attainable? After much thought I decided to take the angle of an outsider telling the story of his quest for the celebrated diva. How was he going to get to meet her and by what means was he going to get her to speak about herself and her career as an operatic singer. The young man's name is François Basil Spirounias, He lives in northern Maine. He's half Greek and half Acadian French. He realizes that his Greek heritage will help him link up with Maria Callas and this heritage considers fine food, Greek food, a tremendous asset. So, he decides later on while in Paris that he's going to tease and delight Maria Callas's palate as an entry to conversations with the diva. Will it work?

François attempts to get a college education in Boston and then he moves to New York City where he is introduced to live theater and opera. With time and money he reaches his goal of getting to Paris. He meets an older couple who lives in the same building on avenue Georges Mandel as Maria Callas. They know her maid, Bruna, and her butler/chauffeur. Eventually François starts cooking meals for the old couple. Then he gradually collects special menus in order to offer a fine dinner to the diva who lives upstairs. With the help of the maid he brings the first meal that he prepares specially for the diva. She is delighted. Gradually François presents evening meal after evening meal and they have long conversations. This leads to their discussing operas, program directors, conductors and other persons who are part of the production. The story unfolds and we discover that Maria Callas is dependent on strong sleeping pills that are smuggled by a close friend as well as her sister. This all leads to her unexpected death and funeral. The fallen Divina is no more and François returns home having ended his quest. Publication date, 2015.

Souvenances d'une enfance francophone rêveuse is a collection of tales and stories published in 2016. When I get tired of writing in English, I switch to French. It's just as easy for me to write in French as writing in English. That's my great privilege as a speaker and writer. It's all part of my marvelous heritage and I am grateful to the Lord and to my ancestors for giving me this gift.

This is a book with 38 tales and stories gleaned from my creative imagination. Thank God I have an active one. The first story deals with my grandmother Laura Beaupré's long hair when she had it cut at the insistence of her daughter, Lena, my aunt. It's a story about the loss of a piece of one's heritage, here the daughter does not understand the loss of Laura's hair that represents her most precious thing in life

Another story is the tales called ***Le Ballon Viné*** /The wine-colored balloon, that tells of the loss of a precious balloon that the little boy had won in a bazaar. He was a poor boy with nothing to his name except his balloon. Unfortunately he loses his balloon. He is devastated at the loss of his wine-colored balloon. He and his grandmother find it, deflated and "dead" as he says. They bury the dead balloon like one buries a dead parent. The boy grieves for the most precious belonging he ever had. Another tale is ***La Symphonie des grillons et des mouches à feu***/The symphony of the crickets and the fireflies. We all know that at night the crickets chirp while the fireflies light up the fields with their blinking of lights. One night there occurs complete silence and people start wondering what has happened to the crickets and the fireflies. It's a genuine loss, they say. The splendor of the nightly symphony of sound and light has disappeared. What must they do to regain this splendor?

It's a testimony to my imaginative mind always at work. ***La Nuit des Oeillets Rouges*/** The Night of the Red Carnations is based on a novel by Marcel Pagnol, ***Jean de Florette*** where Ugolin wants to create an entire garden of red carnations for profit. He has not enough water to keep it growing. He and his uncle find the source of water but it's not on his land. Trouble ensues and Jean de Florette is killed trying to find water. He does not know of the spring on his land and so he uses dynamite to try and find water. A stone hits him on the head and he dies from the wound. It's a two-part story and it's a fascinating tale of greed and lost love. This collection took a lot out of me but once I got started, it was like water flowing gently and endlessly.

My 22nd publication is the life story and works of art of Rosa Bonheur, ***The Day the Horses Went to the Fair---Animal Lover and Painter, Rosa Bonheur.*** It was time for me to write another book on a painter. I chose Rosa Bonheur because she was a woman of great reputation who had astounded the world of art and artists in the 19th Century. She loved animals and painted hundreds of them. She got to be called *une* animalière/ a nature painter or a painter of animals. At first she was not too well recognized for her talent, but the more she produced paintings, the more she became recognized for her skill and he realistic rendition of various animal. She loved horses. She painted several of them until she decided to go to the horse fair in her region. She especially loved the work horses called the *Percherons*, the big, husky horses people used to help them with their work in the field. These are the ones she painted at the horse fair. ***Marché aux Chevaux***, it is called and the very large painting takes up entire wall of the Metropolitan Museum of Art in New York. It was given to the museum by Cornelius Vanderbilt. It sold for 250,000 francs. Bonheur's native city of Bordeaux had refused to buy it at a very reasonable price when offered to its museum.

When I first saw it in New York, I was amazed at its size as well as its composition of horses and men leading them. I later learned that Rosa Bonheur had studied the anatomy of horses and its osteology and that she got into the *abattoirs*/slaughterhouses to really learn the interior composition of horses so that she could paint horses realistically.

"The Horse Fair" is such a striking painting enough to give you chills of amazement and delight. That's what happened to me when I was contemplating the painting. Then and there I told myself I was going to write a book about Rosa Bonheur and her art.

I began to look up information about this artist on the internet and found some cogent material. I tried to find books on her and her life as well as her painting, but there were few of them. I did find out that she had bought an old castle near the Luxembourg forest. It was called Chateau de By. People thought that she was a strange woman since she wore pants, an unlikely dress mode for a woman of her time. She had to obtain a special permit from the *gendarmerie*/police to be able to wear man's clothes. She argued that she needed them to be able to go inside the slaughterhouses.

She had a special friend who came from the States, an artist named Anna Klumpke. For a long time people branded her as a lesbian which she was not.

Eventually Rosa Bonheur's reputation as an artist grew. She was made *Chevalier dans la Légion d'Honneur* by the Emperor and the decoration was pinned on her by Empress Eugénie herself when she visited the artist at her home. This book on Rosa Bonheur and her art is the third work on an artist, all three French. Maybe someday I will write another one, this one on John Singer Sargent that I mention in my book on Émile Friant. Sargent is one of my favorite American artists.

At that point, I wanted to write a book in French and I did not quite know what the subject would be. With time and much thinking, I happen to hit upon a topic that would favor my capacity as a writer and a teacher of folk health care coupled with traditional ethnic values. I had taught a course on that very subject and had traveled to Mexico to learn more about *curanderismo*/Hispanic folk healing. I learned much about the ways and practices of the Hispanic population dealing with traditional health care.

I chose as a topic for my book the life and struggles of a Québécois woman that I named Lucienne. Lucienne is a girl whom people recognize as retarded. However, she is not truly retarded but a privileged person who has a special gift of healing. People simply misunderstood her lack of learning accepted materials in society that measures learning and brain capacity by tests and norms. Eventually Lucienne moves from Canada to New England where she works in the mills. Due to her intellectual incapacities, I have called her the simpleton. The title of the book is ***Lucienne, la simple d'esprit***. Nevertheless, I did not intend in making her out to be a simpleton. It's what people thought she was. She does not conform to norms and she does not meet the standards of society. However, she has talent and that talent is healing. She is Lucienne Lanouette Charbonneau Henry whose heritage flows from a small French-Canadian village called Batiscan. The birthplace of the Lanouette generation. It's an attempt on my part as a writer to deal with my own heritage and the heritage of so many people that emigrated to the U.S. in the late 19th Century early 20th Century. They were hard-working people and many of them toiled in the mills and earned menial wages. Some of them were healers like my father was. Lucienne is the last woman as subject matter for me. Except for another book that I finished writing not too long ago. It's ***La Souillonne et son cat'chisse en images,*** my retired mill worker who talks about her old-time catechism with pictures that was a standard textbook years ago in Catholic schools. It's in process and has not been published yet. I do not know if it will ever be.

There is one thing that I thought of leaving out of this memoir, the major awards that I received. I'm not a braggart but these awards from the French government are something valuable to a Franco-American author like me. They symbolize the validation of the work that I accomplished dealing with important features or dimensions of French culture. Through the efforts of the secretary of the Canadian-American Office of French Speakers, I received from the International Assembly of French-Speaking Parliamentarians in France the medal of *l'Ordre de la Francophonie, la Pléiade* for my work as a Francophone author. Then upon the recommendation of the French Consul in Boston, François Gauthier, I received from the Cultural Ministry in Paris the prestigious medal of *l'Ordre des Arts et Lettres* for exemplary contributions to the French culture. This is where *fierté culturelle* comes into play, cultural pride. I salute you my French heritage and my hard work. Nothing comes without it.

EPILOGUE

Well I'm at the very end of this particular writing and I need to close my story with some thoughts about my writing and the sequel to my memoir, "The Little Eater of Bleeding Hearts". Why the title "When the Flowers Are Gone"? Well, since I had written about bleeding hearts, the flowers of my childhood days, I thought I would link the two writings by focusing on flowers and their metaphorical impact on my life as an author. In the first book, I say that my eating the bleeding hearts as a child meant that this was the metaphor of eating my esthetics. The child eats what he finds beautiful, attractive and charming. He is drawn to these strings of little pink hearts dangling there before his eyes. It's his joy, his delight as a child. It's the splendor of his young days when flowers are in bloom and bring beauty to those who seek it and are ravished by it. Beauty in the child's eye is the reflection of what can be seen, touched and enjoyed by the senses. That's what makes it clearly tantalizing. The esthetics of beauty is incarnate in all human beings. We are drawn to beauty and we delight in it when we stand before a beautiful object, a natural scene, a painting or a sculpture created with talent, or a feeling that warms the fibers of our heart and soul. So much has been written and sung about beauty. I dare not try rival or surpass what has already been written or sung, and I may add painted. There are indeed many venues to capture beauty. For me flowers are the most captivating. I love flowers. I grow flowers. I treasure flowers. Their freshness, their exquisite perfume and their silken soft petals give me the joys of beauty. Oh, the splendor of flowers in bloom. Some may be ordinary like plain grass while others are luxurious things what with their colors and showy blossoms. Of course, it all depends on the way we see things. We can turn ordinary things into extraordinary features of delight because we have the natural talent of seeing things that are transformed before our very eyes. Take the simple and very ordinary *pissenlit*/piss-in-the-bed, the dandelion that everyone dreads on their lawn. Some hate them and do not find them at all beautiful. Others see them as nice yellow flowers that grow to produce little parachutes of seeds fluttering in the wind.

For me, real, natural flowers can always become the metaphors of my esthetics in writing just as the bleeding hearts did in my early childhood days. When the flowers are gone and the winter frost reveals the dormant stage, it's time to recapture the "splendor in the grass" as Wordsworth put it in his long and lyrical poem. There's never a dead season only one that sleeps in the silence and tranquility of seasonal pauses. "When the flowers are gone" is my way of linking or bonding with the two stages of my memoir. The flowers will always be with us, in full bloom or dormant in the soil until springtime. I am glad that I can capture the splendor in the flowers by my writing. It's a good feeling. I once told my wife, "When I die and I'm buried in the local cemetery, don't ever put artificial flowers on my grave, especially plastic. NATURAL flowers only, if you respect my feelings as man and an author." Readers please respect my wishes too. The flowers are gone, the snow is on the ground and the hoarfrost has whitened the twigs that are holding on to the red berries. They are the vestiges of the flowers gone but soon to reappear in the hush of springtime. They return as memories return in the quietude of the mind ever whispering their recall and never to be forgotten. That's what memoirs are about.

Finished May 22, 2020